THE SLANDEROUS SIREN AND THE GRIEVOUS GIFT

A POINT MUSE COZY PARANORMAL MYSTERY
BOOK 5

KELLY ETHAN

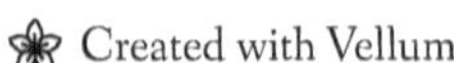 Created with Vellum

A shout out to all those that have helped me with this series.
You rock!!

THE SLANDEROUS SIREN AND THE GRIEVOUS GIFT

A POINT MUSE COZY PARANORMAL MYSTERY BOOK 5

There's a murder in the Playhouse, a vengeful Siren on the loose and a nosy Librarian turned sleuth.
Let the mayhem begin.

After finally agreeing to go on a date with Police Chief and bear shifter, Zach Braun, Alexandra Meyers, aka Xandie, assumed it would be plain sailing.

Not in Point Muse.

Now the Librarian to the supernatural Great Library of Alexandria and her family of Harrow witches have to deal with a new set of problems...

A vengeful Siren, a dead ex-girlfriend, a traveling Playhouse of drama-loving actors and an old nemesis, all with an ax to grind. With bodies dropping at every curtain call, all signs point to Zach Braun as the killer. Xandie has no choice but to swing into Sherlock Librarian mode. Otherwise their first date might be their last...

Can Xandie stop a supernatural apocalypse? Or will things that go bump in the night have her for a midnight snack?

If you like snarky dialogue, murder and mayhem then you'll love the next installment in Kelly Ethan's Point Muse Mysteries, a new cozy paranormal mystery series.

Unlock the mayhem of The Slanderous Siren and the Grievous Gift!

ONE

"She's a murderer." Alexandra Meyers, a.k.a. Xandie, Librarian to the Supernatural Great Library of Alexandria, wrinkled her nose.

"Duh. She lures unsuspecting men in, then...*bam*." Lila Harrow, cousin to Xandie and a witchy baker extraordinaire, slammed her hand down on the Playhouse seat. "She takes them out."

Holly Harrow, part banshee, part witch, and another Harrow cousin, rolled her eyes. "Once upon a time, her siren bloodline may have done that. But the gift is watered down now. Plus, all historical evidence points to sirens luring unsuspecting victims to their side. Any deaths are supposition."

Xandie threw a handful of popcorn at Holly. "Braun is not a victim, but he *is* unsuspecting, or at least oblivious to what that evil..."

Lila shoved Xandie and broke into a paroxysm of coughing as Melody Braun, deputy and younger sister to Police Chief Zachary Braun, ambled up to the cousins.

"Don't stop on my account. Selena Noe is an evil piece of work in my book, even if she *is* Zach's ex-girlfriend."

Xandie winced. Somehow, she always imagined Zach Braun as a newly minted, no previous relationship drama, kind of shifter. Unfortunately, the reality was different from what she'd imagined. According to Melody and her Harrow cousins, once upon a time Zach had a playboy streak. Through high school and right up until he'd left for the Police Academy in Portland and Selena-fake-blonde-siren-Noe. Something happened during that time. An event traumatic enough he'd changed his playboy ways completely. Until Xandie turned up in Point Muse, Maine, he'd barely dated.

"Doesn't seem like he knows that." Xandie scowled and threw a kernel of popcorn at the Playhouse stage where Braun leaned, chatting with his smirking ex-girlfriend.

Melody rolled her eyes. "Please, he knows what she's like. He's just being polite to her. Besides, Zach asked *you* on a date, didn't he? Not her."

"Not that they've made it through one yet. Every time they sit down, he gets called out on police stuff, and the Library sends her away on a research mission." Holly chewed thoughtfully on her popcorn. "Maybe it's fate telling them to give up."

Lila slapped the back of the banshee's head. "Or maybe Point Muse is the crime capital of Maine. Besides, the Traveling Playhouse Company's only here for a few weeks while they perform."

"Too long for me," Xandie muttered. Zach Braun, police chief bear shifter, was a sometimes monumental pain in her Librarian tush. But he was also protective, loyal, and cute in a shaggy blond bear kind of way. Their history of fight and flirt meant Aggie, Zach's mother and police dispatcher, harbored future hopes of bear shifting, Librarian-hybrid grandchildren. But once that siren, Selena, floated into Point Muse, he'd been distracted and moody. And for once, Xandie and the Harrows weren't the cause.

"The saga of your dating life is a source of enjoyment for all of us." Melody snickered, then winced as the fake blonde sauntered up the stairs toward them.

Selena smiled sweetly at Xandie and put a red-taloned hand on her arm. "When a woman gets to a certain age, her thoughts naturally turn to her desperate and dateless status. It's natural. But there are dating sites that can help you. They don't even need a picture anymore. So, please. There's always an option. Don't get anxious," Selena trilled, a musical scale of condescending notes.

Was the blonde interloper using her talent to influence Xandie? If so, why did the siren feel threatened enough to use her vocal gifts? Xandie shook off her claws and smiled sweetly back at the woman.

"Actually, I'm just trying to juggle my work schedule. The Great Library of Alexandria is quite demanding. Have you heard of it?" Xandie tried her own version of a musical laugh but winced as her notes screeched like fingers on a blackboard. "It's so hard to synchronize schedules between a supernatural Library and the police department." Xandie winked at Zach Braun as he climbed the stairs of the Playhouse behind Selena.

"Next time, I leave my phone at home." Zach Braun grimaced, his shaggy sandy-colored hair falling over one eye.

Xandie's sense of order was offended. Her fingers itched to swing his hair back into place. She slid a hand under her legs and pressed hard. "And I'll lock Theo in the Library. No way that cat can open doors and be the Library's messenger then." Theo, Xandie's black feline, was an ancient Greek teenager turned into the Library's guardian, and he delighted in disrupting any romantic plans she had for Zach.

Selena whipped her head around and stared at Braun with narrowed eyes. "How sweet. How provincial." She stepped up to Zach and twined an arm through his. "My boo-boo bear can be hard to pin down. Especially when he has other things on his mind." Selena rubbed her head on Zach's shoulder and smiled victoriously at Xandie.

And on that note, Xandie needed the bathroom before she vomited in disgust at the siren's antics and Braun, just standing there awkwardly, not saying a word. *Or detaching the fake blonde leech from his arm.* She felt the need to gag, violently, in private. "Excuse me, I need to find the bathroom." Xandie stood and shoved her way past the odious duo.

"Oh, I agree, Ms. Meyers. You definitely need to touch up those shiny spots." Selena waved a hand at Xandie's face and grimaced. "The bathroom's backstage. You can't miss it."

Xandie took the stairs two at a time in her haste to leave. She reached backstage and breathed a sigh of relief. "Coward," she berated herself. "Big, bad, Librarian self, and you run away from a mouthy siren."

"She has that effect on every heterosexual woman in the room." A tall, willowy woman with long brown curly hair sat perched atop an old rusted trunk. "Try sharing the stage with her. She's a limelight hog." The woman slid off the trunk and extended her hand. "I'm Emily Roux, understudy to the selfish siren herself. You're Xandie Meyers, the Librarian. Right?"

"For my sins." Xandie shook the woman's hand and then dropped it quickly. She seemed friendly, but if the actress worked with Selena...

"If you're looking for my dark side, don't worry. I save that for her and the leading man. She's a man-eater, so keep an eye on the Chief. She's always dropping little tidbits of their time together." Emily sneered. "Like he's stupid enough to go back a second time. *Unlike my idiot ex-boyfriend.*"

Wow, someone else bitter about the sucky Selena. "I take it you two have history?"

Emily snorted. "I've been her understudy for quite a while. Cornelius, the leading man, and I dated off and on for a year. Until Selena decided she needed his adoration and worship. He dropped me like a hot potato."

"Erm... Sorry?" Really, how did one reply to another's bitter love betrayal?

Emily waved Xandie's apology off. "Karma bit Cornelius on the bottom, so to speak. She dumped him for a mystery man a while ago. No one's seen him, but we see the odd minion now and then."

"She's seeing someone else?" *Xandie should be so lucky.*

"Supposedly. But a siren can never have too many weak-minded admirers." She shot Xandie a pitying glance and held up her script. "Have to get back to the grindstone. She'll jump on any opportunity to get rid of the resident muse and her archenemy." Emily winked and floated off.

Seems like Selena had enemies everywhere. "What a shocker." Xandie peered around backstage. Cruella Selena had mentioned she couldn't miss the bathroom. But as far as she could tell, it was currently invisible.

"I don't care if he's busy. You know he'll take *my* call."

Xandie ducked behind the old trunk Emily had just perched on as Selena stalked backstage, phone clutched to her ear. Seemed like everyone in Point Muse had a spelled phone but her. Because of the ley lines the town settled on, magical feedback disrupted phone communications and discouraged most humans from visiting the supernatural town.

"The family can kiss my booty and so can MMU. Now get him on the phone. I don't speak to talentless lackeys."

Selena's voice trailed off as she moved farther backstage, away from Xandie's hiding spot. Suddenly, her need for the bathroom had gone down the gossip gurgler. "What was the moo she mentioned?" Xandie hadn't realized she'd spoken aloud until Lila leaned over the trunk and peered at a still crouching Xandie.

"The noise a cow makes? Dig this invisible bathroom you found."

Clearing her throat, Xandie stood and brushed her jeans off. "I was talking to another actress, and then Selena popped up on the phone. I didn't want to interrupt."

"You didn't listen to her phone call instead?"

"It was a sacrifice." Xandie shrugged.

"Yeah, well, your sacrifice meant Braun had no reason to stay, and he trotted off with little Miss Manipulative."

Xandie kicked the rusted trunk. So much for their coffee. There went another date.

Point Muse would be a much simpler place if Selena Noe went bye-bye and moved on.

"Apparently he went crazy while he was at the Academy."

An old gray-haired biddy gasped, while her gossipy friend nodded.

"Why are so many of the gossip vultures in Heart's Delight today? Their normal tea and gossip sessions are tomorrow." Xandie snuck another snickerdoodle from Lila's plate of cookie goodies. Christmas in Point Muse was just around the corner, and that apparently meant the all-you-can-eat Christmas Cookie Feast. Festivities in Point Muse equaled yummy goodies.

Lila slapped the cookie out of Xandie's hand. "Now is not the time for a sugar overdose. We have a situation."

Normally that was code for Elspeth Harrow shenanigans. Xandie and Lila's grandmother was an eccentric, wig-loving, hex-mad disaster. But she was still the Harrow matriarch. "What has Elspeth done now?"

"I am innocent of any law enforcement charges." Elspeth plopped down next to Xandie and adjusted her shocking pink, chin-length wig, which clashed with her fluorescent green jogging suit.

Xandie choked on her mouthful of cookie, and Lila thumped her on the back until she dislodged the baked good. "Repeat that again? You're innocent?"

"It's a shock, doll-face, but it has to happen once in a blue moon." Colin, Elspeth's talking pug, waddled up next to Xandie's chair and raised a leg.

Without looking down, she lowered her hand and made snipping motions with her fingers.

"Everyone's a killjoy but my Elspeth," Colin huffed, but he lowered his leg.

A few months ago, Elspeth played with mother nature and enhanced Colin. With a bang and a sizzle, he became the talking, rude, radioactive-gas-releasing dog they all knew...and borderline loved/hated.

Elspeth rapped the table with her knuckles. "As I was saying before the interruption. I am *not* the current feature of the Point Muse gossip queens."

"That's a first."

Xandie hushed her cousins before Elspeth hexed them. There had been a hexed underwear drawer incident a while ago that hadn't been pretty. No one wanted to wear laundry day underwear every day of the week. "So, what—or who's —on the gossip chopping block today?"

"That would be *my* Zachy bear." Aggie Braun, police dispatcher and mother to Zach Braun, dropped into a seat next to Elspeth and sighed. "I knew that woman would be the ruin of him."

Poor Aggie, she looked exhausted. Her broad bear shifter shoulders slumped, and her salt-and-pepper, chin-length hair stuck up in tufts.

"What's going on, Aggie?"

"That piece of work siren. That's what happened." Aggie lowered her voice. "Zachy was in the Academy.

Boston has a supernatural Police Academy there, not to mention the Playhouse Theater next door. That's where he met her." Aggie curled her lip.

"So, they dated for a while?" Xandie cleared her throat. And concentrated on tracing the marks on Lila's well-loved table.

"For a while, but Selena wasn't exactly constant in her attention. She found another mark who would help her career and dumped Zachy flat. She came crawling back, but my boy refused to have anything to do with it. She didn't like that." Aggie chortled.

Poor Braun. No one wanted to be fooled twice. So, why was he hanging on her every word now? "Why is he spending time with her then?"

"Because she asked for help, and he's an honorable soul, but he has no clue she's talking behind his back. Slandering his good name with lies. She's been gossiping with Susie Barnes, and you know what that woman's like."

"The boy is old enough to deal with his own issues. Besides, who believes those loose lips?" Elspeth drew out a hipflask and chugged a quick hit of Witchshine.

"I know my boy's tough. But it's about how people view him in Point Muse and the scuttlebutt she's polluting the town with." Aggie grimaced. "Bear shifters are strong minded, with just as strong a temper. He had a close friend at the Academy. They were rivals in everything, including Selena. Things went badly, and she chose Zach, but there was a fight, and his friend ended up in hospital. They never spoke again. It took him a long time to recover."

"And now she's telling everyone about his history?" What a piece of work. Selena the spiteful was not on Xandie's favorite list.

"Exactly." Aggie pointed a finger at Xandie. "That's

why you Harrows need to shut the siren down. Protect my boy and the Braun family will owe you one."

"Done." Elspeth spat on her hand and extended it to Aggie.

Aggie grimaced but clutched Elspeth's hand and gave it a decided shake.

Elspeth cackled and the lights in the bakery fizzled before surging in a blaze of incandescent brilliance around them.

Lila rolled her eyes. "Cut the hag. My electricity bill won't survive your cackles."

"Fine." Elspeth sniffed. "The girls will head to the Playhouse and have a word or two with that fake blonde menace. And I..." Elspeth smiled wide, dentures on show. "I'll have a close and personal experience with the town gossips. Colin had tuna for lunch, so I'm sure he'll be happy to offload bodily functions on those interfering biddies if they don't cooperate." Elspeth stood and clapped her hands. "Now skedaddle, Harrows. We have a favor to earn."

Something told Xandie that Aggie would end up bitterly regretting the devil's deal she'd just sealed with spit.

***

"A scope would make the spying so much easier."

"Mom, we're just casing the area, no shooting needed...*yet*." Miranda Harrow had just stepped back into Xandie's life after disappearing for twenty years, presumed dead. In true Harrow style, her mom had suffered from amnesia and worked for a human anti-supernatural Black Ops agency, now disbanded, thanks solely to her mother and Paladin Inc for taking them down. But now, Xandie had to adjust to a mother watching her every move.

"I'm so glad we can have a mother-daughter bonding moment." Miranda reached over and grabbed Xandie's shoulder in a quick squeeze before concentrating on the flirtatious siren.

"Yeah, spying on someone's ex-girlfriend bonds a mother and daughter like nothing else." Her mother was slowly readjusting to Point Muse life and her memory was mostly back. Xandie's father still refused to visit Point Muse, but every so often, her mother would head up to Andrews, just outside of Portland, to see him. Xandie shot her mother a quick glance, still surprised every time she saw the woman just how much the Harrow family members were alike. Her mother was tall and muscled, not an ounce of fat. But she still had the Harrow amber eyes that all the women shared. The same stubborn chin and brown hair.

Xandie was average height with sometimes frizzy shoulder-length brown hair. Lila was the eldest and tallest cousin, but she'd inherited curves, long curly hair. Holly, her youngest cousin, was short, with a smooth, chin-length bob. She took after her own mom, Winifred, who was as short as her daughter was. Lila's mother towered over everyone in the family, except for her older sister, Miranda. But they all shared the family trait of amber eyes and a love of chaos and mayhem. Even Elspeth.

"Stop staring. I'm not going anywhere."

"No offense, but you disappeared once before."

Miranda tapped the small of her back. "Mr. Glock loaded with armor piercing silver bullets says I'm staying. Now focus on the mission." She nudged her daughter gently to get her back on track.

Selena's giggle drew Xandie's attention. Miranda had offered to keep Xandie company on her spy adventure as her normal co-conspirators, Lila and Holly, were busy with other duties. Aggie tipped them off that Selena was in Rose Mayweather's bed-and-breakfast bar, sinking a remarkable number of cocktails.

"Can you see who she's sitting with?"

"Only the back of his well-coiffed head. He must've used a bucket load of hairspray to keep that hairdo from moving."

"Not Braun then." *Thank goodness.* Xandie ignored the wiggle of jealousy gnawing at the pit of her stomach. She didn't own Braun. They'd never even finished a date yet, thanks to their busy jobs.

"Whoever they are, they're more than friends."

"Why?"

"Because she can't keep her hands off him. She's eager, and he's playing hard to get. See him angling his body back from her?"

Her mother had superior body language skills. All Xandie had was a supernatural Library, a talking cat, and a knack for finding bodies.

"Since no one has discovered a body here that I know of, I take it this isn't a professional visit?"

Rose Mayweather, bouffant-addicted nineteen fifties housewife and descendant of Greek goddess Aphrodite, tapped her notepad.

Xandie cleared her throat. "Nope, just mother-daughter bonding."

"Then how about you order something and stop spying on that snippy Aphrodite wannabe?"

The not so lovable siren had apparently annoyed Rose, a woman as renowned as Elspeth for holding a grudge. "I take it you don't like her very much?"

"She's a paying customer." Rose leaned in. "But from a

strictly professional view, the way she plays loose and fast with love offends my demigod sensibilities."

Miranda put a hand on Xandie's arm to hold her rapid-fire questions. "Anyone interesting?"

"Someone from the MMU camp. But I don't know who. They always meet at odd times."

"What's MMU?" That was the same sound Selena mentioned on the phone. She'd mistaken it for cow noises. But maybe it meant something else?

"Misunderstood Monsters Unite. It's a family-first political party. They have a candidate taking a run at the North American Supernatural Council."

Miranda nodded. "I've heard about them. They have a lot of ground support and a solid base. A lot of different supernatural species are tired of being painted as the bad guys all the time. Their party leader, Alistair Matthews, has a good chance of being elected."

"Don't ask them where their money comes from though." Rose tapped the side of her nose. "Now what will you have?"

Xandie tore her gaze away from Selena. "Soda for me and something to snack on?"

Miranda held up two fingers and nodded to Rose, who bustled away.

"So, misunderstood monsters are a thing?"

"Witches and mages can get a holier than thou attitudes about pure bloodlines, not to mention all the different deities that muddy the genetic gene pool. Monsters is a catchall phrase. For example, that little siren's classified as a monster. Same with your Chief Braun, because of his bear shifter blood. Point Muse never really cared about that sort of thing. So, both sides flock here because of the ley lines and the neutral feeling of the town."

"Who knew?"

"Speaking of your shifter, I think you have a problem." Miranda nodded over Xandie's shoulder.

Spinning around, Xandie winced as she spotted a harried-looking Braun. "This won't end well." She moved to stand, but her mother yanked her back down.

"Too late." She pointed to where Selena had been sitting.

The siren's date had disappeared, and Braun's ex-girlfriend was flouncing straight toward him, a hand outstretched. "Boo-boo bear. I'm so glad to see you."

Braun brushed Selena's hand away. "You told me to meet you here. That it was important."

Selena cradled her hands against her chest, her eyes quivering as tears trickled out of the corners. "You don't need to be so rough."

Sighing, Zach pushed his hands into the pockets of his work uniform. "I left work for this, Selena. It better not be a ruse just to get me out here."

Gasping, Selena put a hand to her mouth. "A ruse? How could you say that to me? After all we meant to each other."

"What do you want?"

"There are scratches around the lock of my room. When I checked inside, I saw someone has moved my gear around. I want you to deal with it."

"The cleaning staff probably cleaned. You know what a slob you are." Braun turned to leave, but Selena threw herself against his chest, sobbing.

"How can you be so cruel to me? The incident at the Academy proved to me you had a temper, but to turn it on me?" Selena's thin frame shuddered as her wail soared in a musical score.

"Your gifts don't work on me anymore. Remember?" He shoved Selena away roughly and spotted Xandie over her shoulder. "Besides, it's time I organized a date with someone the complete opposite of you."

Selena collapsed against the side of the bar, moaning. "You're a brute, Zachary Braun. It's time the people of Point Muse realize just who the chief of police is and what he's capable of," she screeched when he ignored her and strode over to Xandie's table.

"Incoming, daughter. Prepare yourself."

"Don't tell me, Rose found a body?" Braun stood next to them and crossed his arms, staring down at the mother-daughter duo.

"Not this time, Chief. We're just having a bonding drink."

"Without said drink?" He arched an eyebrow at Xandie.

She pointed to Rose, mincing over to them in her kitten mules with two sodas and some nibbles.

He nodded. "Tomorrow. Lunchtime at the diner. You and me." Braun cleared his throat. "If that's okay with you?"

Miranda kicked her daughter under the table and nodded slightly.

"Are you taking your phone?"

He shook his head. "Miranda can corral Theo. I'm leaving my phone with Aggie. Make sure the Library doesn't need you for an hour or two. Got it?"

Xandie smiled slowly. All thoughts of his conniving ex-girlfriend evaporated from her now barely operating brain. "It's a date, Braun."

Now if she could just have a body-free date...

THREE

He'd stood her up. With their track record, she wasn't surprised. Maybe it was the Harrow bad luck at play? Long-term partners didn't seem to be in the family's cards.

"Don't overthink. He's probably just running late. Trust me, he's over that fake blonde viper." Holly peered at Xandie's shirt. "Is that new? Did Maude get more stock in?"

"It was in her last shipment before she went on holiday. I just got her to put a shirt aside for me." Xandie ran her hands down the sides of her skinny black jeans. The sparkly gray shirt was her nod to dressing up. Being a Librarian who investigated murders didn't lend her wardrobe to haute couture fashion. Not like some fashion-obsessed siren she could mention.

"Anyway. Back to the subject." Holly fixed Xandie with a narrowed stare. "I am here to run interference. Nothing will disturb the Braun-Meyers date. Not work, not the discovery of a body, not a new scroll the Library needs. *Nothing.*" Holly puffed out her non-existent chest. "Banshee on duty." She winked and then hurriedly stood and bolted for the diner counter.

"Banshee and Harrow blood produce strange behaviors."

"Try going to school for years with her." Braun slid into the booth opposite Xandie. "Sorry I'm late. Mom had some things I needed to do first, like delivering a package to Elspeth. I didn't look too closely in case I ended up arresting my mother for illicit substances."

"Deniability is everything." Xandie blushed a fiery red as Braun took a moment to peruse her.

"New top?"

"This old thing?" The clichéd comment made her feel awkward. Xandie gave up the play-act with a snicker. There was just too much Harrow in her blood to play the dating game sweetly. "I bought it a little while ago in case we managed to make it this far."

Zach let out a bark of laughter and reached for Xandie's hand, running a thumb over her knuckle. "That's what I like about you, Meyers. You're honest, no games. If you're annoyed with me, you tell me."

"All the time."

"I spy your banshee cousin at the counter. Is she a chaperone in case I lose my temper?"

A hint of bitterness tinged Zach's tone. Maybe Selena and the rumors she'd spread were getting to him?

She gave Braun's hand a squeeze. "Holly is running interference. Anyone tries to interrupt us, and she'll take them out, banshee style."

"Do I want to know what that means?"

Xandie snorted, all elegance and awkwardness dissipated. "She's a Harrow, so it could mean anything. Best not to question."

Braun slid his hand away and picked up the laminated menu. "Any idea what you want?"

Xandie salivated and gave up all dating decorum. "Turkey melt with fries and blueberry pie à la mode."

Laughing, Braun handed the menu to the waitress who stood waiting next to the booth. "I'll have a cheeseburger with fries and the pie as well. Thank you."

"Coming right up, Chief." The waitress nodded and scooted off to the kitchen where she had a whispered conversation with the cook. She scuttled back to the table. "The meals are on the house on account of you two finally having an actual date and for solving the murder of the old crow who died in here a few months ago."

Xandie laid her head down on the scarred Formica table and let out a hiccupping snort of laughter.

Zach lifted Xandie's head and placed a napkin underneath it. "Don't want bruises on you. The Point Muse world would probably run me out of town."

Sobering, Xandie lifted her head and took stock of Zach. Dark circles rimmed his eyes, and he looked paler than shifter healing should allow. Selena and her poisonous rambling had leached the energy out of him. "How about you confront Selena and ask her to leave town?"

"Because Point Muse is open to all supernaturals who care to visit, and she's done nothing wrong."

"Except spread untruths about you."

He heaved a sigh. "That's the problem. She hasn't. Well, not totally. I was a different person before the Academy. I knew what I wanted, and I fought for it, literally." He dragged his gaze away from Xandie. "I hurt someone who meant a lot to me for nothing. For an image that wasn't real."

Xandie tapped Braun's cheek and made him look at her. "It's called growth. Learn from your mistakes or they'll eat you alive, according to Elspeth."

Losing the melancholy, he grabbed Xandie's hand again. "If it came from Elspeth, then I'd better pay attention. She has a sixth sense for things with teeth."

"Right, here you go." Herman, diner owner and cook, dumped the plates on the table in front of them. "Pie will be out when you're done. Thanks for choosing the diner. I'll scoop the betting pool. Elspeth will fume." Chortling, he waddled off, bald head shiny, his big belly wobbling like a bowl full of jelly.

Xandie groaned. "An illegal betting pool on our first date. Great."

"Point Muse. Always a surprise."

"Boo-boo bear. I'm so glad you're over your little tantrum from earlier. I love my present." Selena pranced up and draped herself over the police chief.

Say what now? Xandie glared at the spiteful woman.

"I got this." Holly rushed up and grabbed hold of Selena's arm, giving it a sharp tug.

Selena tugged back, and Holly collapsed against both Braun and the siren.

"I'm a Harrow. You don't win so easily." Holly pushed away and braced her feet before jerking Selena off Braun.

Selena knocked Holly away and spun to face Zach. "I have no clue who that crazy woman is. But I just wanted to thank you for my gift." She flipped her hair out of the way and jutted her chin out, showing off a sparkly silver chain metal choker.

Braun shot a confused glance at Xandie. "Selena. I didn't send you anything. The necklace isn't from me."

"Of course it is," trilled Selena. "We had a fight, and you said sorry with jewelry. That's how it works."

"Not. Any. More," Braun ground out. "We are *not*

together. In fact, I'm on a date right now." He gestured to Xandie.

"Her?" Selena turned, affronted, to glare at Braun's date.

Oh, sweet karma. Xandie waggled her fingers in hello. "Hi, Selena. Lovely necklace. Not Braun's taste, but still interesting."

"Why you..." Selena lifted fingers in a classic claw-a-girl's-eye-out move but stopped short. She raised a hand to her throat. "It's getting tighter." Selena tried to swallow. She shook her head.

"Are you okay?" This didn't seem like the spiteful Selena behavior Xandie expected. She seemed panicked.

Selena tried to answer but couldn't get any words out. She turned to face Braun and clawed at her throat, eyes bulging. She took a step toward Braun and the table, then stiffened before collapsing, face down in his cheeseburger.

Braun scrambled to find a pulse but eventually shook his head.

Holly stepped up next to Xandie. "That's one way to remove the competition. Poison necklace. Or a hexed one." Holly groaned. "Oh God, Elspeth. Don't tell me this is one of her hexes. Anyone else feel like we're in a wicked fairytale?"

So, what did that make Xandie? *The wicked witch?*

FOUR

"Double hit and keep them coming." Xandie propped her head on her hands and stared at the flames in Lila's old-fashioned hearth.

"Whoa there." Lila held a hand up in a timeout signal. "That's a lot of chocolate powder. Things can't be that bad."

"Braun's ex-girlfriend keeled over dead in his cheeseburger during our first date. Everyone thinks he sent the gift that throttled the life out of her. And now he won't talk to me. Trust me, it's that bad."

"First, Selena only died yesterday. No offense, but murder trumps flirty date talk. Second, no one thinks for a moment he killed her."

Xandie pointed around the bakery filled to the brim with cackling old women. "So why the gossip convention then?"

Lila shrugged. "It's Point Muse, expect gossip. Everyone knows Zach Braun couldn't murder anyone."

A skinny man with no-nonsense, black-rimmed glasses shoved up next to Lila and whipped out a voice recorder.

"Any comment from the Harrow family about Chief Braun's potential involvement in the death of Selena Noe?"

"Are you serious?" Xandie exploded from her seat and shoved her face close to the man's. "Record this. Police Chief Braun would never hurt someone like that. *Ever.*"

Lila hauled Xandie away and patted her back. "Cutting you off. No more sugar."

The man's eyes lit up behind his spectacles. "Xandie Meyers? I'm Percival Hague, a reporter for the Point Muse Chronicles. Care to comment on the torrid love triangle that ended up in tragedy yesterday? My readers are burning with curiosity to know the truth."

So was Xandie. She took a deep breath and murmured a silent plea to the Library for patience. "There was no love triangle. Chief Braun and Selena Noe weren't dating, and we have no clue how she died."

The reporter grimaced and hid his recorder back in his pocket. "I was hoping for more juicy details. But I guess it's too early in your investigation for the Harrow murder instinct to kick in yet."

"What?" Lila and Xandie chorused the word together.

"You know. That thing you do when a murder happens? I wouldn't take too long with this one though. There are a lot of eyes on Braun and not just here in Point Muse either."

People were watching Braun? Xandie's nose twitched. "People outside of town are interested in the chief?"

The reporter scratched the side of his nose. "A newshound is good at digging. And yeah, there are a few interested parties. You're the Librarian, aren't you? Check out Selena Noe's family in your research archives." He winked at Xandie and then blended back into the crowd of gossips.

"Oh, Xandie. I'm so sorry, dear." Susie Barnes, second

biggest gossip in Point Muse and daughter to the biggest gossip, patted Xandie's arm.

She oozed fake sympathy but for the love of Harrow witches, Xandie wasn't in the mood to deal with a nosy woman. "Sorry about what, Susie?"

"Selena's murder. That poor, poor woman. So many secrets. I guess you really never know the true inner workings of a person. Only what they present to you."

"I think Selena was pretty open about being a nasty monster if you ask me."

"Oh no. I wasn't talking about her, but our police chief." Susie lowered her voice. "Selena told me all about it. How the chief was at the Academy, and he stalked Selena until she agreed to go out with him. Even put another suitor in the hospital when Selena showed an interest in him. I'd be very careful around that shifter." Susie pursed her lips in mock sympathy before turning back to her gaggle of gossiping biddies.

"Don't stress. Who knows what poison Selena filled Susie's ears with? You know how gullible she is. She'll believe anything." Lila cleared Xandie's table and placed the dirty dishes on the counter for her brownie to clean.

"I know. But in Point Muse, people think where there's smoke there's fire. People will shun him just on this gossip alone." Poor Braun. The last thing you could accuse the bear shifter of was a violent, abusive temper. Xandie nibbled her lip. A herd of hypothetical imps bounced around the pit of her stomach. She had a feeling about this whole situation. Body count kind of feeling.

"We have a problem." Holly raced up and bent over, gasping.

"Yeah, you need to get some regular exercise."

Ignoring Lila, Holly straightened. "Someone ransacked Selena's dressing room. It's a mess."

Always the damn siren. "What's the problem?"

"Selena's dresser swore she saw Braun near the Playhouse just before she discovered the ransacked room."

Lila waved the brownie, Hester, over to deal with her customers and dumped her apron on the table. "Let's get sleuthing then."

Xandie followed her cousins out of the bakery. Lila was right, they needed to clear Braun's name. Because it was perfectly obvious that the gossips had already convicted him.

"What do we do? The fuzz has Selena's dressing room on lockdown."

"Oh, ye of little faith." Lila patted Holly's cheek. "I'm betting our intrepid sleuthing Librarian has a plan."

They both looked expectantly at Xandie. *Plan?* Selena had dropped dead on their date, so the only thing on her mind was her dating bad luck. Xandie cleared her throat and nodded to the deputy guarding the dressing room. "No Zach, only his brother, Caleb, on the door and his sister, Melody, inside the room with Selena's dresser. So, we need to distract them and then wing it." She shrugged. "That's all I've got. Take it or leave it."

Lila puffed up her hair and adjusted her top lower. "A girl's gotta do what the sleuthing calls for." With a flick of her hair, she strode toward Caleb Braun.

"She looks more like Mata Hari than Ms. Marple. We probably won't have a lot of time." Xandie dragged Holly behind a corner and peered out, waiting for Lila to do her thing.

"Hey, Caleb." Lila leaned against the wall.

"Lila." Caleb peered around, searching for something.

"What are you looking for?"

"Your partners in crime." He grimaced. "Zach would kick my furry behind if I let Xandie get involved."

"Hey, as far as I know, Xandie isn't standing in front of me." Lila arched an eyebrow. "I can just leave. If you don't want your mom's message, it's fine with me."

"Why would she give you a message when she could just radio me?"

"So suspicious, Deputy Braun. All I know is she said reception was on the fritz in the Playhouse. And for you to head across the road for further updates. Told her I'd give you the message. It's up to you if you listen." She stepped back and shrugged.

Caleb coughed. "I'll head across the street and check. Can you stay

and let Melody know what's going on when she comes out?"

"Sure." Lila waited for Caleb to disappear and frantically motioned her cousins over. "Quick, we don't have a lot of time."

Xandie knocked on the door. "Won't Aggie drop us in it when he talks to her?"

Lila scoffed. "Please, what am I? An amateur? It's all worked out."

Melody Braun opened the door. "It's about time. I couldn't delay any longer. Hurry and get in here. You've got five minutes." She shoved past the women and into the corridor.

"I'll stay with Melody."

"Thanks, Lila." Xandie entered the room and the trashed and deadly quiet atmosphere hit her. "What a mess."

"He really tore this room apart. All her pretty things ruined." A tiny redheaded woman sniffled as she stood in the corner.

"You're Selena's dresser, right?" The poor little thing appeared distraught. Her face was pale with shock, causing freckles to stand out like tiny red stop signs.

She nodded compulsively. "I've been with her a few years now. I love being part of the theatrical world."

"Did you like working for Selena?" As Holly entered the room, Xandie motioned for her to start checking out the area. "I mean, I heard she was difficult to work with."

The woman exploded, all grief gone in the wake of her vehemence. "That was pure jealousy. She was a brilliant actress. The more talent you have, the more temperamental people see you as. It's a rule or something. I wouldn't expect you to understand her."

Bitter toward Xandie or what? "What do *I* have to do with it?"

"She mentioned Chief Braun all the time and this Librarian hanging off him. She laughed about it. Selena knew you couldn't compare to her. She thought you had dirt on him to make him run after you." The little woman sneered at Xandie.

"No dirt. Just mutual respect and liking. Unlike Selena." Xandie walked around the small room, hoping something would stand out as a clue. "You know who I am. But you haven't told me your name."

The tiny woman scowled. "Polly Harper. Not that it's any of your business. Since the man who probably killed Selena is running the investigation, I guess it doesn't really matter what I tell you. That bear shifter will cover everything up, anyway."

Xandie gritted teeth. "Braun is honest. He would never hurt anyone or cover it up."

"That's not what Selena told me. In fact, she told me she didn't want to come to Point Muse at all. She wanted to avoid the shifter. But she had no choice."

And pigs flew. "Then why was she all over him every time he ran into her?"

"He convinced her he wanted to get back with her. The shifter even sent her a gift." Polly grabbed a box and threw it at Xandie. "See? Even has his name on it as the sender."

Holly was right, the box had his name on it, but it didn't mean he'd sent it. Xandie glanced at Holly, who was picking through paperwork on Selena's makeup table. "Is there anything missing in here? Do you know?"

"Not that I can tell."

Polly's hand drifted to her pants pocket for a moment as if she was reassuring herself that she hadn't lost something.

"You okay there, Polly?"

She dropped her hand away from her pocket. "Except for the fact a close friend was horribly murdered? I'm fine. If you'll excuse me, I need to leave." Polly shoved past Xandie and out the door.

A thump and a curse outside the door had Holly and Xandie rushing out of the room.

Polly and Melody had tangled with each other, and the tiny dresser had come off second best.

Melody reached out a hand to the fallen woman and yanked her upright. "Sorry, didn't see you come out, little one.

"It's fine." Polly patted her pocket, freezing as her hand

came up empty. She dropped to the ground again and scrambled for a plain handkerchief that had fallen out.

Lila got to it first and picked up the handkerchief. "Is this what you're after?" She held it out.

Polly snatched it and hid the handkerchief away. "Thanks. Don't take this the wrong way, but I hope never to see Point Muse again." On those parting words, she stormed out.

Xandie frowned and took a step forward as a flicker of movement caught her eye. A dark figure slid farther back into the shadows until it disappeared. *Interesting.* Someone watched Polly collide with Melody. *And* saw Lila pick up whatever Polly had dropped. The mysterious watcher disappeared as soon as Polly left. So, who was watching Selena's dresser and why?

"Right, you guys skedaddle before Caleb's back. Any leads you get, let me or Aggie know. We won't let Zach go down for that nasty piece of work's murder." Melody nodded at her friends.

Surely that wasn't even in the cards? "Braun can't be a suspect. He's the police chief."

Melody winced. "It's all about the evidence, but he had a pre-existing relationship with the victim. And we're hearing some pretty nasty rumors about higher-ups interested in this case. Now get out of here before you're caught."

Xandie placed a hand on Melody's arm and whispered, "I thought I saw someone hiding in the shadows watching. Keep an eye out, just in case."

Melody nodded and shooed them out with a flap of her hands.

The women headed out the back of the Playhouse.

"Well, well. That was interesting," Lila drawled as they

skidded to a stop around the corner from the Playhouse and away from Point Muse law enforcement.

"What's interesting?" Other than the fact somebody spied on Polly.

"That handkerchief I handed back? There was something in the center. It felt like a heavy bracelet, and knowing Selena, it would have been expensive."

Xandie frowned. "Why couldn't the bracelet have belonged to Polly?"

"If it was hers, why not wear it? Why hide it in a handkerchief and then panic when you lose it?"

"True, so she must have snatched it from Selena's dressing room. But why take it?"

"That's not the only thing I found." Holly held up a slip of paper and some paperwork.

"A bus pass?"

"You can read, Lila. You don't need to make a guess." Holly shook the pass at her cousin. "This is a pass for the MMU rally. Misunderstood Monsters United? And this is her paperwork. All signed and approved by the head honcho himself, Alastair Matthews."

Why would Selena, singing drama queen, be interested in a political rally?

Unless she was more interested in the politician himself? A rich politician who may have liked to give expensive bracelets as gifts... *Or a choking necklace?*

"We might just have our first suspect."

FIVE

"The gift box sent to Selena had poor Zachary's fingerprints on it."

"What?" Xandie paused outside Lila's bakery, Heart's Delight, and stared, shocked, at her Aunt Winifred. "It can't have. He didn't send it to her."

Winifred clapped her hands, and her dyed, blood-red hair bounced on her shoulders. "Aggie got me a message. Some sharpshooter from the big smoke's coming in to run the investigation and has stood Zach down."

"That's ridiculous." Xandie's last word exploded out of her mouth. "He's been set up, framed. Railroaded by someone with an agenda."

"Unfortunately, we don't always see the flaws in those close to us, Ms. Meyers." A tall skinny man in an expensive suit with slicked back, black hair bowed to the ladies. "Apologies for interrupting you. I couldn't help but hear what you're discussing."

"There's no way our police chief could commit murder. No way at all." Xandie crossed her arms and glared at the interrupting stranger. "How do you know my name?"

The stranger held out his hand. "George Perse. At your service."

Xandie reluctantly shook the man's hand, wincing at his too-tight grip.

George released her hand with a quizzical glance. "The Librarian to the Supernatural Great Library of Alexandria is famous in our world. As soon as we knew we were campaigning in Point Muse, I decided to introduce myself. Bit of a fan."

Library groupie. There was a first time for everything. "Campaigning?"

He handed her a campaign button. "*MMU.* Misunderstood Monsters United. We're in town for a rally."

MMU. The pass for Selena that the head of the political party, Alastair Matthews, had signed off on. "I heard MMU was campaigning here." Taking a punt, Xandie dropped a verbal bombshell. "Please tell Mr. Matthews we're thinking of him at such a terrible time. Few people will mourn Selena, but I know they were close." Xandie threw the bait out and waited for the fish to nibble.

He quirked an eyebrow. "What makes you say that?"

Xandie waved a hand airily. "Oh, you know what Point Muse is like."

"Full of gossiping biddies," Winifred butted in and blinked her eyes coquettishly. "I'm Winifred, Xandie's aunt. It's nice to meet you."

George Perse inclined his head but still focused on Xandie. "Selena's family are big supporters of MMU, especially as they're sirens. But Mr. Matthews has only met Selena Noe briefly. They're passing acquaintances."

"Oh?" Xandie affected surprise. "Maybe I'm wrong. I thought they were close. I guess a distraught person will do or say anything when they're out of their mind with grief."

"My impression was the only person Selena Noe was close to was herself. Especially since she was only visiting Point Muse and not a long-term resident."

"Her dresser at the Playhouse is mourning her. And maybe Mr. Matthews and her family. Who knows who'll come out of the woodwork for her funeral?" Xandie shrugged. "Now if you'll excuse me, I just realized I have somewhere else to be." Xandie linked arms with her aunt and ambled off down Main Street, away from the bakery.

"Why aren't we going to the bakery, Xandie, dear?"

"Because I just realized he was right. Selena was only visiting Point Muse. She was staying at the Mayweather Inn." Xandie waited for the words to sink in.

Winifred clicked her fingers. "And you haven't searched her room yet?"

"Bingo. I'll head there now. Can you call Holly, see if she can meet me there?"

"You can rely on me." Winifred snapped a salute and hurried off in the opposite direction.

Xandie just hoped they were in time to search before the police tracked down Selena's room. Braun needed all the help he could get.

***

"You might need this."

A grayish-white key dangled in front of Xandie as she peered at the lock. "Do I really have to use Great-Aunt Rose's finger bone?"

"Well, it *is* a skeleton key." Elspeth cackled, and the inn's hallway lights surged and hissed.

"Remind me again why you're here?"

"Just being helpful. Holly and Winifred are distracting Rose. I came to help my favorite granddaughter turn over a murder victim's room." Elspeth beamed at said granddaughter.

"Call it family bonding, doll-face." Colin scratched his ear with a paw. "Plus, she's bored, and you know how that ends."

In jail. "Fine. But no crazy antics. We're in and out. Got it?" Elspeth on a hex-mad rampage was terrifying enough, but a bored Elspeth was DEFCON runway.

"Deal." Elspeth gently pushed Xandie out of the way and opened the door with her aunt's finger.

Shuddering, Xandie followed a prancing Colin inside the room. She pointed at the dog. "Hear me, pug. We all know what your bladder's like. No pee stops here, got it?"

"Got it, *mon capitan.*" Colin tried to salute with a front paw but tipped over instead. "Whoa, someone moved the floor."

Elspeth shoved a can of hairspray at Xandie. "Spray your hands and don't miss any skin."

Xandie took the can gingerly. Who knew what Elspeth had stored in it?

"Don't be a baby. It's a spelled sealant, so we won't leave our fingerprints in the room. I sprayed Colin's paws as well."

Giving in, Xandie sprayed both hands, then gave the can back to Elspeth. "We need to find anything that points to another suspect. We both know Braun didn't do this, we just need to present another option to the cops." Xandie wandered around the room and ignored Elspeth and Colin. The room wasn't ransacked like Selena's dressing room at the Playhouse, but it definitely wasn't clean. Selena had been a slob.

"Oh geez. Get it off. Get it off," Colin whimpered as he shook his paw frantically.

Xandie bit back a snicker as Colin danced around the room on three legs, pitching into anything in his way.

"My poor baby. What has that nasty dead woman done to you?" Elspeth flew to Colin's side, her long, neon-blue wig flying as she plopped heavily next to him. Cooing, she grabbed a bright yellow sticky note stuck to his paw and yanked. She made kissing motions at the abused paw. "Poor little Colin. Nasty sticky note hurting my little man."

Xandie shuddered at the image of her dangerous, and slightly devious, grandmother gushing over a talking, cigar-smoking, radioactive-gas-passing dog.

She peeled off the yellow note now stuck to her grandmother's fingers and frowned as she tried to make out the writing.

"MMU. Five pm, backstage." Nothing to explain who was meeting whom, except for the initials MMU. And MMU stood for Misunderstood Monsters Unite. But why meet with Selena? Surely if this was a meeting between Matthews and Selena, the note would have sounded more personal? Deciding to work on the puzzle later, Xandie pocketed the piece of paper.

"Keep going through the room. See what else we can find. Some evidence that might implicate someone else. We need to offer the police another suspect."

Nodding, Elspeth patted Colin and then kept moving around the room, cackling every so often as she ran a finger over some of the siren's trashy belongings.

Ignoring her grandmother, Xandie wandered around the tiny room. Clothing covered every available surface, but not in a ransacked way. More slob than tossed. The top of a small desk in the room's corner was full of receipts for jewelry, makeup, and clothing. If she had a mystery man, Selena had been milking him dry. Xandie rifled through the papers, but most were receipts. Until she came across a wad of hand-printed notes. Something about them tweaked her curiosity.

She read aloud the topmost note. "Stop poisoning Point Muse." Then she picked another one at random. "Stop gossiping or you'll regret it." She slid out one from the bottom of the pile. "Don't air dirty laundry. Now you pay for your sins."

Xandie arched a brow at Elspeth. "Selena was getting threatening notes. Could the guy she was dating have sent them?"

"Any names on the nasty grams?"

"Just an initial. Z. B." Xandie closed her eyes. *Zachary Braun.* No way Police Chief Zachary Braun, the most uptight, annoying, by-the-book law enforcement officer and bear shifter alive, would send his ex-girlfriend threatening notes and place his initials on them. At least the Zach Braun she knew wouldn't. Xandie gathered the notes together just as Colin howled. Spinning around, the notes in hand, she stared as the door slammed open and a tall, dark, muscled figure stood in the doorway.

Colin shrieked like a little girl and ran behind Elspeth, a radioactive cloud of nervous flatulence spreading from the quivering dog.

Xandie pressed a hand over her mouth and nose. The pug wasn't known for his bravery or physical prowess, unless it involved rescuing Elspeth. Every time the poor animal became terrified or ate tuna, he let loose with the most foul-smelling belch of gas ever smelled on the goddess-blessed earth. Xandie tried not to breathe too deeply as she waved her hand in front of her face to direct the cloud away.

"Who are you, and why are you standing in my crime scene?" the interrupting stranger said with a deep voice.

His crime scene? Xandie tried to hide the papers behind her back.

He strode over to Xandie and pointed his finger. "Why don't you drop the papers into this handy evidence bag." He opened a bag and held it up. "I'd hate it if I had to arrest a member of the public for contaminating a crime scene."

Huffing, Xandie drew out the threatening notes from behind her back and dropped them into the plastic bag. "Yeah, that's the worst thing that could happen in Point Muse. Care to explain why this is *your* crime scene?"

Elspeth hoisted Colin onto her hip, her neon wig flowing behind her. "Point Muse is getting all the hot male specimens lately." She winked at the big, brawny man while a panting Colin nestled on her hip.

The gentleman reared back as Colin's stench floated over to him in a wafting cloud. "I'm Detective Scott. I'm here to investigate Selena Noe's death due to a conflict of interest with the police chief. *I repeat.* What are you doing in the victim's room?"

Zach was in big trouble if the higher-ups had brought somebody else in to investigate the murder. And she'd just handed over incriminating letters to the lead investigator. Stepping up, Xandie forced a smile. "I'm Xandie Meyers, the Librarian. Wasn't sure if the police knew if Selena had a room here, so we thought we'd check it out first, then let law enforcement know. We have some experience in investigations."

"Ah, Xandie Meyers. Are you interested in this room because you're dating Police Chief Braun?"

"*One date.* One date we never even finished. And as for the conflict of interest? Zach Braun would never hurt anyone, let alone an ex-girlfriend."

"Trust me, Braun has enough hidden anger to do anything. Out of this room right now. And stay out of my investigation. If I catch you poking your Librarian nose into this matter or any of my crime scenes again, I'll arrest the both of you." He pointed to the door. "Please take that ripe animal with you as well."

Elspeth narrowed her eyes. "Careful what you say about my baby. No one wants an underwear drawer that seals itself shut." Elspeth cackled, and the windows rattled in their frames.

Growling under her breath, Xandie pushed Elspeth and a panting Colin out of the room. She spun around in the doorway and stared at the man. "I have no clue who you are and no wish to get to know you. But the Library considers the Braun family friends, and it responds to threats. Watch your step."

"I'd suggest you don't threaten an officer of the law, girlie." He moved closer to the doorway. "Just remember, I'll be keeping an eye on you. I've already checked up on you, and the scuttlebutt is that you've helped to solve murders before. So, if you *do* happen to find any evidence, I'd like you to get in contact immediately." With that, he reached into a pocket, extracted a business card, and handed it over.

Xandie took it with bad grace and shoved it into the pocket of her jeans without even looking at it. Then she stomped off and followed a cackling Elspeth down the stairs. She just hoped that man paid attention to her warning and thought twice about railroading Braun into a murder charge. She had a horrible feeling Harrow bad luck was about to hit the Braun clan and Point Muse in an epic way.

<hr>

Rose Mayweather, inn proprietress, self-styled nineteen fifties housewife, and descendant of Aphrodite, stood at the base of the stairs. She spotted Elspeth and Xandie and motioned secretively for them to follow her into her office. She slammed the door behind them and pressed her back against it, shutting the Harrow, Meyers, and pug trio in the room. "Thank Aphrodite you're here."

Xandie arched an eyebrow. Rose grateful they were here? Had the underworld frozen over? "Is there a problem?"

"A big one. The police will turn up here any moment. This is the tip of the scandal that will send my inn under."

"Get with the news. The fuzz already busted us searching the siren's room. Trust me, we know the police are here."

"You don't understand, Elspeth. Have you even heard about that man?"

Xandie would certainly like to know as much gossip about Detective Scott as possible. "I have no clue who he is, do you?"

"He's a detective from Portland. He knows all about Braun and Point Muse and is here to oversee the investigation into Selena Noe's death."

"What does he know about Zachy bear?" Elspeth dropped Colin on the ground, and he sprawled at her feet, tummy heaving.

"Apparently, those two have a history and knew each other in Portland. And there's no love lost between the two of them." Rose leaned in with an expectant expression on her face. "That's all I know. He brought his own administrative staff and deputies. The Braun clan are on temporary leave. And issues were raised about Police Chief Braun's actions and connection to Selena Noe's death."

Dammit, exactly what Xandie feared might happen. The last thing Zach Braun needed was removal from his post. His family had policed Point Muse for decades. "Why tell me?"

"Because you're the Librarian and you're nosy." Rose rolled her eyes. "Plus, the cleaner contracted to clean the police station overheard the new staff gossiping. I thought you'd want to know since you're the one dating Zachary."

"One date. Interrupted by a dead ex-girlfriend."

Rose threw her hands up. "Whatever. But someone dying who is connected to my inn is bad for business. And that Selena Noe was the worst possible victim. Too many secrets. Particularly that family of hers."

Gossip. "Selena's family?"

"Siren mafia. Her family controls all the sirens in North America. They have deep pockets. She was a black sheep, but she was still part of the family. The Noes aren't famous for their compassion and empathy. They're going to want their pint of blood from whomever murdered her. And they won't care what Point Muse residents and businesses get in their way. I don't want my business to end up as collateral damage just because that woman picked a quality place to stay."

Elspeth nodded. "I've come across a few of the family before. Nasty pieces of work. And if I'm saying it, it must be bad. They particularly like to dabble in politics."

"MMU. Misunderstood Monsters United."

Rose nodded. "Exactly. Her family are major donors to

MMU. Find out what's going on, Xandie. Aphrodite knows I can't stand any of you Harrows. But I need your help." Rose opened the door and ushered Xandie and Elspeth out. "I'd prefer it if you could be more incognito next time. I don't want any more people knowing you're investigating *my* inn." The woman grimaced at the thought.

Xandie rolled her eyes. Even while asking for help, Rose couldn't stop from flashing her disdain of the Harrow family. "No worries. We'll be discreet."

Elspeth chuckled. "Hear how good she lies? Xandie gets that from my side of the family. Discrete?" She giggled again.

"Speak for yourself, Elspeth." Xandie bit her lip. She needed to work out exactly what was going on. But first, she had to speak to Zach and get his side of the story.

Even if I dread the answer.

SIX

"I wonder if Aggie has her hot tub up and running." Elspeth slapped her leg and cackled as she stared at the massive wooden lodge the Braun clan of bear shifters owned. "Last time Aggie hosted our poker party, everyone ended up in the hot tub." She hooted. "All that wrinkly skin on show and nary a swimsuit in sight. We nearly drank the town dry. Best hangover I ever had, and I didn't even need to cheat at cards. Good times." Elspeth sighed.

Xandie shook her head. The less she knew about her grandmother's antics at her poker club, including naked family members in a hot tub, the better. At least for her mental health. As far as she was concerned, her grandmother's poker parties were calm reflective gatherings where absolutely no chaos and mayhem brewed. "We're just here to talk to Zach and his family. Find out what the heck is going on and what he wants us to do. And Elspeth? No antics. No hexing. Just questions and answers. Simple and easy. Got it?"

Elspeth rolled her eyes. "Easy is my middle name. Don't stress. Worry gets you lines on your forehead. If you don't stop obsessing, Xandie girl, you'll end up looking like a senior citizen before you're in your thirties. In fact..." Elspeth leaned forward and poked Xandie's forehead. "You already have a couple. Might be time to consider a potion or two. Life is meant to be enjoyed, Library Girl."

Losing interest, Elspeth nudged Colin with her foot. "Come on, boy. Nasty, flesh-eating shifters might be in the woods. Let's get your cute little bottom inside, unless you want to end up as an appetizer."

"Doll-face, I'm not an appetizer. I'm the main dish. They should be so lucky to taste my fine canine body. Besides, I can handle shifters any day." Even as he denied his worry, his tiny paws moved at top speed as he trundled along the stone path. Elspeth trotted behind.

Xandie took a moment to consider how she should phrase her interrogation of Zach without upsetting their burgeoning relationship. They'd agreed to go on a date recently, but with both of their work commitments taking over their lives, they'd only managed to have a sit down together the day of the murder. *And* a body had ended up in his cheeseburger. Not the greatest start to a meaningful rela- tionship. Speaking of which, she had no clue exactly what their status was. So, how she handled asking questions about his dead ex-girlfriend was kind of important. Xandie sighed and waved as Aggie stood at the end of the porch and hollered.

"If you're coming in, hurry up. You have a choice of a comfy porch chair or the couch inside. And if you're quick, a hot chocolate or a cup of tea. Move it, Librarian."

Xandie smiled. Aggie Braun, police dispatcher, bear shifter, and mother to the Braun clan, was one of her favorite people in Point Muse. Aggie was a tall woman with a grizzled, gray, chin-length bob. Reputation as a sharpshooter, fiercely loyal to family and friends, and always there in a pinch when you needed her. *And a crony of Elspeth's.* Xandie climbed up the porch stairs and slumped onto a chair. The massive house the Braun family had built sat on acreage including a dense forested area that backed up to their lodge. "This place is amazing, Aggie. Serene. Plenty of land for some shifters to run free." Xandie winked at Zach's mom.

Aggie leaned back in her rocking chair and grinned. "It is that, Librarian Girl. Built generations ago by Braun ancestors who came across from the Black Forest in Germany. They wanted somewhere secluded, so we have a lot of acres, and we back onto the National Forest. Even have a creek stocked with fish for the fishermen amongst us." She patted her rocking chair arm. "My husband carved this rocking chair, just for me. He thought when I was old and gray with grandchildren running around, I'd need to rest my tired bones on the porch and watch them play." She arched an eyebrow at Xandie.

Xandie fought a wave of red that flushed her cheeks. "One date. I keep telling people, one date. And it ended up with a body in a cheeseburger."

"Selena Noe. She was always bad news. The day he met her in Portland, I warned him she'd ruin his future. Now here we are."

Elspeth narrowed her gaze on her friend. "We'll find out what the heck is going on, Aggie girl. But we need to know the full story. Why is Zachy bear being railroaded into a murder conviction?"

"Someone's out to get him. We know that much. One of our contacts in forensics gave us a heads up. The Playhouse dressing room had Zach's fingerprints all over it. Same as the necklace that suffocated that damn woman to death. He swears he wasn't in the dressing room and he never gave the gift. They also found prints on the box that had the necklace in it, but he never gave her the gift."

"How did his prints get there then? You and I both know he didn't give her the necklace any more than he killed her. Someone's gotten hold of his prints. How?" Xandie gritted teeth. There was no doubt in her mind Braun was innocent of this. So, what was the motive? Frame Zach and get him out of the way? Why Braun and why kill Selena?

"That's just it, Xandie. We have no clue. We're as much in the dark as you guys are. All I know is that some bigwigs cleared us out of the station, along with anyone else who has connections to the Braun family. Put us all on administrative leave. The bigwigs are now doing an internal review of Selena's case and any other cases in the last few months that Zach was involved in. Zach's future could be at risk."

Not to mention his freedom as well. "How is he coping? I haven't seen him since the date. And that was a few days ago."

"Sensitive, moody, and grumpy. That's about the size of it." Melody Braun wandered out the front door and plunked on the porch next to Xandie. She shrugged. "After Portland, he wasn't much of a party animal, but now he's holed up in the house. Whenever he goes out, the gossiping biddies point the murder finger at him. I can't understand how quickly Point Muse turned on him."

"I believe you, kiddo. But he's a bear shifter, and he kills things and eats them. He's got these razor-sharp claws and…"

Xandie shoved a hand over Colin's rambling mouth. "Yeah. Try not to help anymore."

Colin sniffed his disdain. "You say that now, chickie.

But we both know who you'll come to when you need some help. And it ain't that fake feline or that weird old Library."

"What is it with you and Theo? You're both driving me crazy. When are you going to settle down?"

"When that mouthy kitty admits he's not real and I'm not a freak of mother nature or a pugenstein. I'm manly, I have magnetic attraction. I gotta fight the girls off."

Melody snorted. "It's not magnetic attraction, it's your bodily functions, and they're fighting to get *away* from you, so you don't suffocate them."

Xandie cleared her throat. "Can we not talk about Colin's unfortunate bodily functions?"

Aggie giggled. "Always count on a Harrow to provide a little light relief. Let's go inside. Getting chilly out here."

Xandie followed the others as they strode into the Braun bear shifter lair. *What a warm, well-loved house.* She realized she'd spoken aloud when Aggie agreed with her.

"Like I said. Built by Braun hands. Our family takes pride in our workmanship. Most of the materials you see here came from the old country, the Black Forest. There's a lot of history in this house."

Xandie marveled at the workmanship in the entryway which opened into an immense living room. A large worn rug partially covered the wooden floorboards that were scarred with decades of bear shifter claws. Comfy worn couches ringed a huge stone hearth. A cathedral ceiling made the room feel even bigger, and thick beams framed a large, open-plan dining room with a massive table and mountainous chairs.

Xandie turned and had a look at the kitchen which opened onto the dining area and sitting room. Gleaming stone counters and creamy white cupboards framed a huge silver fridge. A large, sweeping staircase ran from the corner of the main living room up to the mezzanine floor with multiple doors off it. Xandie soaked in the feeling of warmth and love. The house was built for a large family. It needed bear shifter children running everywhere.

Melody pointed up the stairs and to the left. "Each of us has our own wing. The house is huge. Lots of bedrooms. Every generation adds to it. Not to mention multiple bathrooms." She rolled her eyes. "With three bear brothers who like to spend time in the shower, it's nice to have my own bathroom."

Xandie pointed to the tapestries on the walls. "Are those bears supposed to be your clan?"

Aggie nodded. "One of our family members commissioned another bear shifting family in the area to weave the tapestry so we wouldn't get homesick for the Black Forest. Brauns have had a good life until now."

One would think the massive amount of polished wood in this house would overpower you, but the rustic warmth called to Xandie. Large gable windows at the end of the main room let a ray of sun in. Double doors opened onto another covered porch at the back of the lodge. The porch faced a grassy area and a large flowing creek. Nature up close and personal. Nice and secluded if you were a bear shifter wanting privacy. She pointed to the creek. "Aggie mentioned there's fish in there."

Melody nodded. "Zach loves to pull out fish, then throw them back. He spends most of his time out here in the summer. We can get a fair amount of snow up here in winter. We're off the beaten track, even though Point Muse is only a ten-minute drive away. And with the National Forest behind us, we don't really have any neighbors nearby."

"Did someone mention fish?" Colin licked his lips. "I'm not a fake feline

who craves seafood, but now and then isn't too bad."

Elspeth shook her head and waggled a finger. "No fish. We all know what that does to your insides."

"Party pooper." The pug stalked away, collapsed in front of the fire, and dropped off to sleep in the space of a heartbeat.

Elspeth, hands on hips, spun in a circle, and her bright pink, curly, shoulder-length wig bounced with her. "Right. We need Zachy bear. We need to find out what the heck is going on, and we have little time to do it."

"How about I speak to him, and you speak to the twins? See if they know anything." Elspeth would barge in and put Zach's bear hackles up within a second. Best she spoke to his twin brothers. Zach was the eldest of the Braun siblings with Melody the youngest. The twins, Caleb and Riley, nudged in between as the middle children. They squabbled like anything, but when one of them was in trouble, they backed the other one to the hilt. The siblings shared the same muscled shoulders, shaggy blond hair, and piercing blue eyes. The three younger siblings were more light-hearted than Zach, but all the Brauns were protective of their friends and family.

Elspeth rubbed her hands in glee. "Bring on the boys."

"I can't wait to see how this goes." Melody giggled and scampered off to grab her brothers.

"They're playing pool. They fear Elspeth, so they'll tell her anything. Zachy's a little harder to intimidate." Aggie held out a hand. "Come on, Librarian Girl, let's go find my eldest."

Aggie led Xandie through a door onto a covered porch and down some stairs out onto the land at the back of the lodge. A cool wind blew, and Xandie shuddered. Christmas was still some time off yet, but there was already a chill in the air.

Aggie pointed at a figure sitting on a rock next to the edge of the creek. "That's his thinking rock. He always goes there when he needs to work things out. Speak to him. See what he says."

Xandie nodded her thanks and waited for Aggie to disappear back inside the house. Hopefully he would speak to her, because they needed his help to solve this mystery. She wandered over to Zach and sat down next to him. Trailing a finger through the icy cold water, Xandie hissed and yanked her hand back. "Well, I won't be doing that again. That's icy."

Zach shot a small smile at Xandie. "The creek's fed by the mountain stream so it's freezing. We bears don't really notice the cold. The temperature's fine for us. Our bear hide protects us so we can go fishing whenever we want."

Xandie shuddered at the thought of fishing with a bear. That probably meant eating fish raw. She leaned back and lifted her face to the pale sun, taking a moment to compose her thoughts.

"I know what you're here for. So, spit it out, Meyers."

"Maybe I just wanted to visit Braun lodge?"

Zach took a page out of Xandie's playbook and snorted. "You are insatiably curious and can't help yourself when it comes to a murder investigation. You want answers."

"All I want to know is who is framing you."

"No question about whether or not I killed Selena?"

"Of course you didn't kill her. Like Elspeth, if you had, no one would have found the body. Your mother and my grandmother are fully capable of hiding any corpse or evidence from the authorities. That evidence was found means you didn't kill her."

Braun broke into Xandie's words. "She collapsed dead in my cheeseburger. That's impossible to hide."

"Doesn't matter where she died. Elspeth would know if you'd killed her. Then she probably would have black-mailed you. You're innocent. Now we need to know who benefits from framing you. Any ideas?"

He shook his head. "I have no clue who'd hate me that much. I just don't know."

"Elspeth and I had a quick look around her room at the inn, but we didn't have long before the cop busted us."

"You need to stay out of this investigation, Xandie. I know I seem to put this on repeat, but you can't get involved. Stay out and let whoever's investigating deal with it. I don't want you in danger." He placed a hand on Xandie's shoulder for a moment before removing it and going back to staring at the creek.

"I'm not staying out of the investigation. It's just not going to happen. Make use of the Library and my catalyst abilities. Otherwise, you'll find yourself railroaded into a cell permanently. "

"Fine." Braun sighed and rubbed a hand through his untidy hair. "You found something in Selena's room. And judging by your expression, it wasn't good."

Xandie sighed. "I found two things. A yellow note stuck to Colin's paw that detailed a meeting, time, and the initials MMU. The other was a series of threatening letters signed with your initials."

"I haven't corresponded with Selena since our Academy days. We didn't part well, but that doesn't mean I hated her enough to send threatening notes and murder her."

"I know that. But you're being set up. By someone who

knows you well or has researched your background with the siren."

"You mentioned you only had time for a quick look. Why was that?"

Xandie wrinkled her nose. "Some new police guy busted us. Some guy your higher-ups brought in to oversee the investigation. Didn't seem thrilled to find us nosing around. He collected the letters from me, then kicked us out."

"You were contaminating the crime scene. I would have evicted you too. I'm sure whoever is investigating will follow the evidence. The Library might have some background information, so don't forget to check in with it. Anything else?"

Xandie nodded. "Yeah. We got into the dressing room and had a good look around. Selena's dresser seemed a bit squirrelly. Was definitely covering something up. When we left the room, she dropped something out of her pocket. Lila found it, told me it felt heavy, like jewelry. But I noticed someone hidden in the shadows watching the whole time. The new investigator hadn't turned up yet, but I mentioned it to Melody."

Braun hunched over his knees, resignation in every line of his body. "At least you mentioned it to Melody. I can't keep you out of the investigation but trust the justice system. Whoever's heading the investigation will find the truth."

"We'll see." Xandie switched gears. "Tell me about your past with Selena and the gossip she spread around town."

"I was an idiot and let hormones cloud my judgment. I ruined an important friendship and hurt somebody I cared about. That's all you need to know."

"Trust me. There's more to it. Details now."

"When I was at the Academy, I had a best friend. We were both competitive. Friendly rivalry. One of us was always top of our assessments. Then we met Selena. There was a Playhouse next door, so we saw a lot of her. I guess she chose me, and it didn't go well. I let my emotions override my logic. I lost control, and my friend ended up in the hospital."

Zach paused and dragged in a deep breath before continuing. "Selena told me about my friend pursuing her, not taking no for an answer. Jasper was interfering and scaring her, so I dealt with it, and he ended up in the hospital. Afterward, some acquaintances let slip they'd seen Selena with someone else. I confronted her, and she admitted that she was seeing the director from the Playhouse. *The married director.*"

He shook his head, amazed at his own stupidity. "Once Jasper was out of hospital, he left and finished the Academy in a new area. Selena took off with her director and I came back to Point Muse. A little while later, she contacted me, wanted to come back. My answer made her furious. She didn't handle the rejection well."

"Not exactly a shocker. Do you have any contact with Jasper?"

He shook his head. "Haven't talked since that day he ended up in the hospital. I tried to call, but he refused to speak to me. Has every right to hate me. As far as I know, he joined law enforcement after graduating and is doing pretty well. I can't see him being the one to kill Selena."

"Somebody did. If you don't let me investigate, you'll end up in a cell. We can't let that happen."

Braun stood and carefully helped Xandie up. "Ask about her family. Selena always dodged questions about them. I know Paladin Inc has investigated them more than once. Buchanan's pretty much living at Harrow House now. Maybe get some information from him?"

Xandie nodded. Buchanan was an old Paladin Inc handler. He'd been friends with Elspeth and her husband, Lucas, when they were young and before Xandie's grandfather was killed in an explosion at his headquarters. Buchanan came to town a while ago as a handler for one of Elspeth's ex-coven members. Sadly, the coven member died, and Elspeth was implicated.

The Paladin agent had helped the Harrow family and Xandie protect Elspeth and clear her name. He'd stuck around, and these days had a flirt/fight thing going on with Elspeth. Surprising, considering Elspeth had a pathological distaste for anything law enforcement or Paladin related. But her grandmother readily admitted Paladin agents were hotter than normal run-of-the-mill police officers. Paladin Inc had more far-reaching powers of protection than any other justice department. The agency had formed centuries ago and dealt with supernatural, worldwide Armageddon events.

As they mounted the steps to the back porch, Xandie heard Elspeth cackling. "What now?" She walked into the main room to see Zach's twin brothers bent over retching. Melody Braun stood on the other side of the front porch door, giggling. Xandie clapped a hand over her nose and one over Braun's. She mumbled behind it.

He shook his head. "I can't hear you."

Xandie opened her fingers a little bit so he could hear her words. "Someone gave Colin fish."

Elspeth rolled her eyes. "It's a natural bodily function. Everyone's a drama hag." Elspeth waved a hand around to dilute the thick green cloud that hung in the air. She poked a groaning Colin with the point of an iridescent sneaker.

"The bucks here had no worthwhile information, so we need to get back to the Library and research. Your mother and Buchanan will meet us there. We need to end this before it interferes with my next poker game."

Xandie dropped a hand away from Braun's face and waved it in front of her own to clear the noxious fog.

"Remember what I said, Xandie. Stay safe. Let the Library help and keep in touch. Okay?"

Xandie nodded. "Will do. And you remember, no stiff upper bear lip attitude here. You find out any information, you share." She nodded to him and trotted out after Elspeth.

Time to talk to the Library.

SEVEN

"Look what the hag dragged in. About time you turned up." Theo, Xandie's black cat and Library guardian, hissed his displeasure as Elspeth dragged Xandie into the Library.

"Investigation, remember? I told you where I was going."

Theo hissed again and stalked over to the Library desk and jumped up on it. He batted at a pile of notes. "Obviously, the Library didn't know where you were, and it's got work for you. Just look at this mess." Theo waved a paw around.

Originally, the Great Library of Alexandria had been a supernatural repository of all knowledge within their world. But a demon-possessed Julius Caesar tried to gain entrance. Once refused, he'd burned the Library down. Theo, a.k.a. Theophilus, was a Greek teenager at the time. His father had been the current Librarian but had been out at the port, supervising a shipment of new scrolls. Theo had lurked in the stacks and read scroll porn while sipping from an ancient hipflask. Julius Caesar had firebombed the Library, and to save him, the Library had transformed Theo into an immortal feline guardian. He provided a conduit between the Library and the Librarian down through the ages.

Xandie's family had made guarding and protecting the Library their duty. She'd inherited the position from her Great-Aunt Sera. Theo plagued Xandie every day. Although she wouldn't readily admit it out loud, she couldn't imagine being in Point Muse without her mouthy furry feline. "I'm here now. If there's an issue, I can sort it out. Stop whining, Theo."

"Whining?" Theo hissed and pushed paperwork off the desk onto the floor.

"That's mature for an ancient guardian."

"I take my cues from the company I keep." Theo jumped down and pranced haughtily around the room with his tail in the air.

Xandie took stock of the room. The old house in which the Library resided was deceptive. In the style of a colorful Victorian mansion, the house was, in fact, small inside, with only the main sitting room, dining room, kitchen, three bedrooms upstairs and what appeared to be a tiny Library off the side. The Library had a second entrance that had outside access. But once inside, it was more like the TARDIS. Bigger on the inside than it looked on the outside. The tiny bay windows looked out onto a large garden with rickety wooden stairs down to the cove below. Internally, the Library had dark wood shelves filled with ancient books and scrolls dotted about the room, with a small office and stationery room to the side.

Small tables, lounging chairs, and reading seats filled the room. Plenty of space to spread out if the Library let someone in to do research. Part of Xandie's job was to note down appointments in the book. The Library would decide who could access her information and write the invitation in the book for Xandie to send out. If the client was denied physical access, then Xandie would copy the research needed and send it out. Occasionally, the Library refused any access, and details written in the appointment book were erased.

The number of people who tried to access the Library for nefarious purposes was ridiculous. Every time a new book or scroll or any information written about a supernatural creature appeared in the universe, it ended up in the Library. Xandie's job was to file every scroll and every text in the appropriate area.

Thankfully, her previous job as a Librarian at Andrews College Library, and working under her father, had prepared her. She'd already had Library experience and loved the smell of a dusty old book and running her fingers over every spine, just wondering what information was inside the book. So, working in a supernatural Library suited her. Unless the Library and its feline guardian got antsy.

The Library had an almost childlike nature and loved to make mischief. Xandie snagged floating, dueling scrolls out of the air. She shelved the offending scrolls back into their correct positions. She glared at her mother and Buchanan, who'd snuck in and were sitting on the couch watching Xandie and Theo's antics. "And why has my mother and Elspeth's main squeeze and semi-retired Paladin agent graced us with their presence?"

Miranda smiled. "We thought we could help with your investigation."

"Help? Or interfere?" Xandie narrowed her gaze on her errant mother. Miranda Harrow had disappeared twenty years ago. Essentially, a *Sanguis Pura Equis,* a pure blood knight, had hunted Miranda off a cliff. Obsessed with racial purity, they searched out those who polluted the human bloodline. Unfortunately, Harrow witch blood counted.

Xandie had been five when two knights had tracked them down. Her mother had distracted them and let Xandie escape. The killer knight had then run her mom off the cliff. A merrow, or mermaid, named Coral had saved her mother's life and deposited her up the coast in an obscure fishing village. Her mom, unfortunately, had amnesia, and the flighty merrow hadn't thought to let anyone know who she'd snagged from the sea. Until a few months ago, everyone thought Miranda had died. Everyone except Xandie's Great-Aunt Sera, who'd hired Herman, a troll private investigator, to find any information he could about Miranda. And he'd found a lot.

Her mother had worked as a Black Ops agent for the Anti-Species Project, or ASP for short. A human department of the government that, like the killer knights, focused on pure blood humans and eradicating supernatural creatures. Without a memory, Miranda Harrow had no clue she was hunting down those of her own kind.

When she started regaining her memories, she disappeared and sought out the Harrow family, coming to her own mother's rescue when an old connection from Elspeth's coven tried to kill her. Now, she was permanently back in Point Muse and in Xandie's life again. Her mom's memory was almost one hundred percent back, and the holes were filling up quicker than anyone had hoped for.

Paladin Inc had helped Miranda escape from ASP, and Miranda appreciated the irony of turning on the group and using her skills against their ideals. The group had disbanded, thanks to help from Paladin Inc and Buchanan. The grizzled old Paladin was surprisingly entertaining to be around.

Especially when he fought with Elspeth. Everyone ate popcorn and sat back to enjoy the fireworks. Lately, the fireworks had been flirty as well. Xandie shuddered. He spent more time at Harrow House than Xandie did. Nice to see Elspeth finally moving on after years of being a widow. As long as Xandie didn't have to think about what they did behind closed doors, it was all good.

"Help only." Miranda winked. "I know you're a grown woman with her own instincts. The Library wouldn't rely on you if you couldn't take care of yourself. It just takes a little while to adjust since the last time I saw you, you were a little girl of five."

"In that case, I need all the help I can get."

"Between your mother and my Paladin contacts, we may be able to dig up some intel that will get that bear shifter off a murder charge."

"You don't believe he did it?"

Buchanan snorted. "Please, that choirboy? Mighty bear shifter, with the nasty claws, doesn't have the killer instinct. Elspeth on the other hand..." He nodded at Xandie's grandmother.

Elspeth cackled, and Xandie gritted her teeth, waiting for the lights to fizzle. Thankfully, the Library was strong enough to withstand her haggish powers. It was a pain changing light bulbs every time Elspeth blew one. It was a curse to be on the wicked witch's clean-up crew.

"What a compliment." Elspeth winked at her beau.

Xandie ignored her grandmother's antics and focused on her mother. "Off the top of your head, do you have any intel on Selena or the MMU?"

"I've had a few dealings with Noe family members. Both with ASP and through Paladin Inc. They're a family to handle carefully."

"You aren't the only one to say that. The new detective warned me off, and Braun's concerned, but I'm not stopping until I clear Braun's name. So, her family?"

Miranda nodded. "Family of sirens. And very strong ones. Some lines are diluted, but the Noe family is fairly pure. They've consolidated their clan and built it up mafia style. There have been various investigations into their criminal activities. Basically, they're magic proof. Every charge or investigation seems to flow off them and nothing sticks. Money laundering, blackmail, protection racket, race fixing. You name it, they do it. And they have no compunction about eliminating loose ends. Watch how you step, baby."

Heat pooled in the pit of Xandie's stomach. It had been a long time since she'd heard that endearment out of her mother's mouth. Maybe Xandie wasn't as grown up as she thought. She focused back on the investigation. "Remarkable kind of family. Selena bucked the mafia family and became an actress and musical star. But did she cut ties completely or did she spy for the family? The Supernatural Playhouse plays theaters all around the supernatural world. Selena traveled to a lot of different countries and had access to different people. Did she slip her family information?"

"I never met Selena, but you don't ignore the Noe Family. I definitely see her passing information on from various towns, politicians, rich benefactors, or companies that she dealt with. Not to mention any contact with law enforcement agencies. The Noe Family would love a police officer in their pocket."

"That ain't Braun. Aggie would never forgive him if he did that. She'd clip him around the head." Elspeth sauntered around the corner of the couch and dragged herself over to a leather chair.

"Never fear, Colin the superhero is here." Colin bounded into the Library

and snuggled underneath the table next to Elspeth's chair. He knocked Horatio to the ground, drool dripping onto the chittering imp's head. "I'm exhausted from solving all your problems. It's good to see you lay food on for these briefings. I needed a snack."

Theo hissed and barged under the table, nose to nose with Colin. "Leave Horatio alone. He is *not* a snack. Weren't you just in the kitchen clearing out our pantry, anyway?"

Horatio, the hairless imp in a bright orange velour tracksuit with his name bedazzled on the back, scooted underneath Elspeth's leather chair, chittering wildly. He lifted a tiny fist at Colin, who tried to shove his head under the chair. Theo yowled and jumped on Colin's back.

Letting out a plaintive cry, Colin ran around the Library, bucking like a rodeo horse. But Theo stuck to his back like outraged feline glue, his claws sunk in. The cat's tail dangled under the dog as Theo's back legs bumped against Colin's bottom.

"Get. Him. Off. Me. I swear I'll go pug on his fake feline whiskers. Get him off me. *Now.*"

Buchanan coughed, hiding what sounded suspiciously like a snicker. He reached down and snagged Theo off the pug's back, putting the cat on the couch between him and Miranda. He frowned at the dog. "I'm sure Colin has had enough to eat. *And* he knows that Horatio is not on the menu. Unless he wants to go on an imp only diet?"

Colin shuddered. "What a traumatic threat to suggest to a well-meaning pug. But message received. Just tell that animal to keep his claws to himself." Colin scrambled to Elspeth and shivered against her legs.

"My poor baby. Was that mean Paladin threatening you?" Elspeth leaned over and placed Colin on her lap, smoothing kisses all over the dog.

Xandie gagged. Baby talk for that oversexed, always hungry, flatulence-ridden animal was bad enough. But watching her grandmother smother the animal in skin-touching kisses was more than she could deal with. "Please, can we get back to MMU, Selena Noe, and murder?"

Buchanan agreed. "I can call in some favors. Get intel on the lead detective. Miranda said ASP investigated both MMU and the Noe family before. She might be able to find something more on them. And Paladin Inc is more than happy to work with the Library and the Librarian. Unlike other agencies, we don't discriminate."

Miranda agreed. "I'll hit up my contacts. I still have a few in the business. And I must head to Portland anyway to see your father. I'll combine my visit with a few meetings with my contacts."

Her father had never moved on from her mother's disappearance. He'd buried his head in the sand and blamed Point Muse and its supernatural residents for her loss. To see her back among the living was a huge change for him. He had hated Point Muse since her supposed death. Even before Miranda's disappearance, he'd hated the weird that was Point Muse. Great-Aunt Sera had raised him after his parents had passed away. Being raised in the strange world of the Library had been more than he could stand. He still refused to set foot in the Library, even though her mother was back.

Her mom visited him every few weeks. Xandie had no clue as to the status of their relationship. The less she knew, the better. But she must admit her father seemed happier when she spoke to him on the phone. Hopefully, that meant he'd get off her back about leaving the Library and Point Muse. "Right, I think that's a good starting point. If you can both speak to your contacts and get any kind of information, that will help. Meanwhile, I'll research the Library for information on Selena and her family. Get more of an idea about what they're like. Have any of you heard about MMU?"

"Only by reputation." Elspeth smirked. "That political organization isn't at my level of chaos and mayhem, but they're still interesting. Full of misunderstood monsters, apparently." She sneered, then scratched under her wig before continuing. "Anyone classified as a monster is welcome to join. Any creature possessed or cursed, you name it, MMU will take them in. Power in numbers, I guess. All I know is it's Alastair Matthews' party. He controls it with an iron fist. Sometimes he uses stand-over tactics, and they're a tad shady on the way they bring in their donations." Elspeth shrugged. "That's all I got. I'm sure Miranda and Buchanan could find out more information than I can. Unless you want someone hexed. Then I'm your hag."

Elspeth shoved Colin off her Lap. "Right." She pointed to Miranda and Buchanan. "You need to vamoose, *now*. You both have your jobs. And I need to go back to Harrow House and brew a few protection spells. Just in case you break open a hornets' nest."

Miranda gave Xandie a quick hug. "I won't stop you. This is your job, and I know how much Zach means to you. Just be careful." She nodded and dragged Elspeth out the door, Colin trotting behind.

Theo shuddered and slid Horatio out from under the chair. He flicked the imp up onto his back and flounced up to Xandie. "You'll have to do another grocery run. Because we both know that four-legged, Elspeth-engineered monstrosity has cleaned us out of food. Hopefully, he left my tuna alone this time." Theo poked his nose in the air and pranced out of the Library.

Buchanan rose slowly and stared at Xandie for a moment. "I'm glad those three have left. Adds a little peace to the room, don't you think?"

"You were holding out. What information do you have that you didn't want to talk about in front of my family?"

"Alastair Matthews. The head of MMU. Take care in your dealings with him."

"Not you too. I've had all the warnings I can take. *Seriously*. I can understand Elspeth going on about do-gooder genes and people's helpful advice now."

"I'm not giving advice. Trust me, that won't work on any of you Harrow women. Say nothing in front of Elspeth or Miranda. I've had dealings with Alastair Matthews and his family. He has a reputation with the ladies and for getting what he wants. Paladin Inc. has investigated his family and not just for blackmail. People disappear around him. Especially those who stand up to him. Lucas, your grandfather, crossed paths with Alastair's father, and it didn't finish well. One of them ended up in the hospital, the other in jail. Didn't take too long for Lucas to recover. But Adrian, Alastair's father, went to jail and died in his cell soon after. No cause of death discovered. Alastair has always had a grudge against the Harrow family. That includes you. Alastair had no choice but to step up and get a job when his father died. He went to the Noe family and they floated him. He's been in bed with them ever since. Tread lightly."

"Great, somebody else with a grudge against the Harrow family. I'm getting used to the enemies the family seems to accumulate. MMU stands for Misunderstood

Monsters United. So, what kind of monster Is Alastair Matthews?"

Buchanan smiled at Xandie like a proud parent. "Good question. He's a charisma mage."

"What's monstrous about that?"

"He's a descendant of Calypso, who's the daughter of a Titan. Qualifies him as monstrous. Don't mess with the Titans, and that includes their descendants. Calypso was a powerful monster who could sing her victims to sleep before killing them. She also used to weep alone. I can't see Alastair doing that. But his voice can charm people into doing what he wants. Like I said, he has a reputation for burying people who stand up to him—financially, socially, and physically. You need to be careful."

"So everyone tells me." Xandie patted the grizzled Paladin agent on the arm. "If it makes you feel better, I won't do anything that the other Harrows wouldn't do."

"Not so much." Buchanan shook his head and turned to leave. "Just keep in mind what I said. Not everything has to be handled alone."

Before Point Muse, she would have scoffed at his words. But now, meeting the Harrows, she was starting to believe he was right.

All for one and all that jazz.

EIGHT

"Murder is good for business." Bodies packed Lila's bakery to the proverbial rafters...and not the dead kind. Xandie waved at a few faces she knew, but most were strangers.

"Not murder, politics." Lila motioned Xandie behind the counter. "Most are MMU supporters. They're taking a cookie break, apparently. I even had to call the dragon in." Lila pointed to Es Penne, teenage rebellious dragon shifter.

A few months ago, Es and her family had been embroiled in a murder frame-up scheme that could have ended tragically. Thankfully, with Harrow and Meyers help, they'd found the culprit, and Es had gained Priss, a long-lost older cousin. "MMU is more popular than I thought."

"MMU isn't the draw card. That hunky silver fox is." Dorothy Johnson and her sister-in-law, Olive, stood at the counter and giggled.

Xandie fought her gag reflex. The two women, hairdressers and sometimes naked dancing witches, were in their eighties and as man hungry as oversexed barracudas.

Olive, sporting an emerald green beehive hairdo, patted

Xandie's hand. "Alastair Matthews is a very dashing politician. Sister and I aren't MMU designated party members, but we do like listening to him speak."

Dorothy sighed dreamily. "Shame about the wife."

"He's married?" Maybe the wife had found out about Selena and Matthews and exacted her revenge?

Olive nodded toward a back table where two men and a stylishly dressed, raven-haired woman sat sipping tea. "Emma Matthews. Socialite and part dryad. She's in all the gossip magazines." Olive leaned closer and mock whispered, "If you ask me, she's a cold fish. That sort only gets passionate about trees and nature."

Xandie glanced casually around the room. Emma Matthews was a stunning woman, but she definitely seemed disinterested in all the surrounding chaos. In fact, she was staring out the window and ignoring everyone. Not exactly the scorned woman driven by jealousy to off her love rival. "How long have they been married?"

"Ten years next week. They don't have any kids, but Matthews' platform is monster family issues. It's very important to him." Dorothy paid Lila and then turned to Xandie. "We just want you to know, dear, that we support you."

Huh? "Support me in what?"

Lila made a cutting motion at Dorothy and groaned when the hairdresser ignored her.

"Why, in your fight to prove poor Zachary Braun's innocence."

Olive nodded and chimed in. "We don't believe for one second he killed that trollop. If it had been Elspeth, though..." Olive winked. "That's a different story. But if you need help investigating, just ask. We love murder mysteries."

Dorothy fluffed her blonde pixie-cut wig and slid an arm through Olive's. "On that note, it's time to depart. We heard a rumor that Alastair might need a trim before the big rally. We need to set up the salon just right. Toodles." The old woman waved, and the scary duo disappeared out the bakery door.

Lila shuddered. "I don't know who's worse, them or Elspeth. If they weren't so talented with the chop and dye, I'd avoid them like the plague." She fluffed her curly brown hair that sat in a bouncy cheerleader ponytail. *"Good hair just don't care."*

"I take it the entire town knows we're investigating?" Shouldn't surprise her. Gossip in Point Muse was a gold medal sport.

"Duh." Es Penne slammed an arm full of dirty cups and plates down on the counter. "Everyone knows what the Harrows and the Librarian are like when it comes to murder. Add in the betting pool on your date, and you're a hot topic."

"Great. My love life is a financial gain for someone else. That's just perfect." Xandie grimaced and sagged against the counter. It was hard enough to deal with first date jitters, then a dead ex-girlfriend, a potential murder charge against her boyfriend, and now someone making money off her love worries. The gift of Point Muse never stopped giving. "Maybe I should move?"

"Too late." Lila shoved a plate of tiny green cakes at Es. "Take this to that politician and his wife. Apparently, she'll only eat green foods."

Es backed up a few paces and shook her head. "Nope. Not me. I stay away from anything MMU and especially that man."

Interesting. Someone who didn't think Matthews was a

goddess' gift to monsters. "Your family are dragons. Surely you qualify for MMU membership?"

"Yep, we're monsters all right." Es bared sharp, pointed incisors with a smirk. Then she sobered. "Gran hates the guy. He and his aide turned up to the compound a few times in the last week, to press the flesh and secure a donation or a public declaration of support. But Gran refused to see him."

Marjorie Penne was a cantankerous dragon and a poker crony of Elspeth's. Not to mention very wealthy. Gold and knowledge were her hoard. So why refuse to meet with the politician? "Why wouldn't she meet with him?"

"Matthews likes to put the whammy on people and get them to do what he wants. Gran likes to be in control, so no whammy for her." Es shrugged, her long black hair with a single stripe of white rippled behind her. "Plus, he's backed by the Noe family. They've scuttled a few Penne business ventures before. As far as Gran's concerned, run with the sirens, swim with the fishes. I'm not taking their food over. Find another sucker."

"Right." Lila took the plate back and shoved it at Xandie. "Deliver with a smile and pump them for information." She gently pushed the groaning Xandie out from behind the counter and toward the trio in the back of the bakery.

Putting her Sherlock Librarian face on, Xandie smiled as she deposited the cakes onto the politicians' table. "Here you go. Sorry about the delay, but Lila's very busy today. Break time for MMU?"

George Perse nodded appreciatively as he gently pushed the cakes at Emma. "MMU has numerous supporters. We're excited to help support, both physically and financially, Point Muse businesses." He cleared his throat.

"Mr. Matthews, I'd like to introduce you to Alexandra Meyers. The current Librarian to the Supernatural Great Library of Alexandria."

Alastair Matthews lifted his silver-streaked hair and smiled warmly. His emerald green eyes glittered at Xandie. "It's such a pleasure to meet you, Alexandra. I've heard fantastic things about the Librarian and her Library." He took Xandie's hand and held it between two palms.

Oh eek. The politician was literally pressing her flesh. Thankfully, there were no babies around to kiss for a photo opportunity. "It's Xandie, please. And don't believe every-thing you hear." She slid her hand out from between his and wiped her leg, a smile still firmly attached to her face.

Confusion wrinkled the politician's forehead for a moment before it smoothed out. "All complimentary, I'm sure." He turned to his wife and tapped on her shoulder to get her attention. "Emma, dear. This is Xandie, the Librarian."

Emma looked up from the green cupcake she nibbled on. Hazel eyes underneath smoothly coiffed raven hair stared uncomprehending at Xandie. After a few seconds, the woman frowned, and a spark of life lit her face. "I met the previous Librarian. She was lovely and helped me find information on oak tree propagation. I was sad to hear about her death."

Out of the trio at the table, Emma appeared the most genuine. So, why was she married to a consummate actor like Matthews? "Thank you. That means a lot. Murder's a tragic thing to deal with, but I hope she can rest easy now." Xandie smiled at Matthews' wife. "If you need anything else, please contact me. I think we received new horticul-ture scrolls just a few weeks ago."

Emma nodded and looked pleased before the spark

drained out of her again and she went back to nibbling on her cake and staring vacantly out the window.

"Excuse my wife. She's not comfortable on the campaign trail away from her gardens."

George interjected. "But Mrs. Matthews is always happy to support her husband."

Sure she was. "It's just so sad that Point Muse hasn't been painted in such a good light since you arrived." Xandie faked a grimace. *Here, fishy fishy...*

"Ah, the death of that poor siren. Such a sad event." Matthews nodded solemnly and George Perse joined in.

"I passed my commiserations on to your aide. But I'd like to offer them personally to you. From experience, I know what a toll murder takes on the loved ones left behind."

Matthews stiffened, as did George, on the other side of Xandie. That was all the reaction she needed. Alastair Matthews definitely had some kind of relationship with Selena.

Matthews recovered and frowned at Xandie. "George passed your sympathies on, but I must admit I was surprised. The only contact I've had with the late Miss Noe was of constituent nature. And her generous family are large supporters of our campaign."

Big guns time. "Really? I'm positive I saw you only a few days ago, having drinks with Selena at Mayweather Inn?" Matthews' pupils contracted and then dilated. Xandie did a mental victory dance. He hadn't liked the fact she had seen him with Selena. So why meet in such a public place?

"Just a constituency meeting. Nothing personal."

George butted in and tapped his watch. "You must excuse us, Xandie. MMU works on a tight schedule."

And the man wanted to run away from what Xandie's questions implied. She took a quick glance at Emma. The woman was oblivious to the questions and the undercurrent of the surrounding conversation to the point the men talked freely in front of her.

Matthews smoothly took Xandie's hand again and stared into her eyes, his voice melodious as he spoke. "I'm sure you want to do whatever you can to protect your police chief. But I can assure you, I had nothing to do with that woman's death. I would never jeopardize my standing with MMU." He gripped her hand tighter. "Nothing can interfere with the cause. *Nothing.*" He let her hand go and looked expectantly at her.

Xandie cleared her throat. "I must've been mistaken. Enjoy your cakes." She nodded at large to the table and pretended to bustle around other diners in the area. The two men looked shocked and had their heads together, furiously whispering, completely ignoring Emma Matthews. Why so surprised? Was it about her reaction to his words? Matthews wanted her to back off the questions, so she had. Unless her reaction wasn't quite what he'd expected. In the Library pow wow, someone had thrown around the words *charisma mage.*

Maybe Matthews' press of the flesh had accompanied a charisma whammy. Except, thanks to the Library and possibly her Harrow blood, she was immune to spells, hexes, et cetera. Poor little politician probably didn't know what to do.

Matthews' phone rang, and he excused himself to stand in an empty corner of the bakery to answer it.

Xandie slowly wove her way closer and pretended to wipe something from underneath the table as she eavesdropped.

"I told you not to call me directly. Everything goes through my aide." Matthews paused, then growled into his phone, "I know what the stakes are and who you lost. But I warned you about her. It's not my fault you can't control your own family."

Someone from Selena's family had just called Matthews directly... And they weren't pleased.

"I know what my responsibilities are. You don't have to remind me of your strings. Next time, ring my aide." Matthews disconnected the call and took a calming breath before smoothing his hair back into place as his wife and aide joined him.

Xandie kept her floor post as she watched them leave. Someone in the Noe family was keeping the politician on a short lead, and he wasn't happy about it. Just how far would he go to get the monster mafia off his back?

The bakery door flew open and slammed against the wall. Holly rushed in, her chin-length bob in wild disarray as she huffed to a stop. "Xandie. Alert. Alert," Holly squealed and raced to Lila, grabbing her cousin and shaking her. "We have to find Xandie and warn her."

"Hecate's toenails, calm down. What's got into your banshee blood?"

Holly took a shuddering breath. "The fuzz is coming for Xandie. Aggie tipped me off."

Xandie stood or tried to. She'd forgotten she was crouched under a table. Wincing, she rubbed her abused head and scooted back before standing. "Who's after me?"

A tall figure blocked the sun out of the bakery's doorway. "That would be me. Detective Jasper Scott, internal affairs."

She frowned, her mind going into overdrive. Hang on.

Jasper? Didn't Braun call his long-ago friend Jasper? *Unusual name...*

She dug into the back pocket of her jeans and pulled out the business card the detective had given her when she'd searched Selena's room at the inn. And there it was in black and white. Detective Jasper Scott. Coincidence? Not likely. No such thing as coincidence in Point Muse.

So, this is Braun's Academy nemesis...

NINE

"Do your dates normally end in murder?"

Xandie sat opposite the tall, good-looking police officer in Lila's bakery kitchen. Her cousin's island bench was the perfect height for a police interrogation. "It was a first date. And bodies are an occupational hazard in Point Muse. Doesn't mean either of us murdered somebody." Xandie glared at Braun's nemesis.

"Except all the evidence points to Police Chief Braun. Including his fingerprints on the murder weapon and the box."

Two plainclothes deputies stood behind Xandie's interrogator, arms crossed, glaring. She pointed to them. "Do we really need the goon squad?"

Detective Scott gestured the policemen out of the room. "This is a serious matter, Ms. Meyers. No one wants a dirty cop running a station. Particularly not in Point Muse."

Xandie gritted her teeth. "I told you. He didn't do it. Someone's framing him."

"You don't think he has it in him to kill?" Scott threw a

handful of photos onto the counter. "Does that look like someone who wouldn't hurt a fly?"

Xandie chanced a quick glance at the photos. They were of a young man, face turned away from the camera, but the bruising around his jaw and cheek bones was obvious. She knew exactly who these photos were of. "Shouldn't you excuse yourself from this case? With your prior issues, surely that makes you biased?"

Scott gathered the photos and tucked them away. "It's not about what I feel, it's about the evidence. Braun's fingerprints are everywhere, including on the murder weapon. What can you tell me about the victim?"

"You mean Selena? The same Selena you both fought over years ago? I would think you'd know more than I do." Petty to bring it up but satisfying to score a point over Scott.

The detective pinched the bridge of his nose. "Yes. That Selena. I'm sure you've seen her around town."

Xandie snorted. "I've run into her. Sweetness and light, she was not. More like sneaky and manipulative. *And* she was badmouthing Zach around town. She might have faked wanting to get back together, but she was definitely seeing someone else."

"Any idea who?"

She hated to give any of her sleuthing info up, but if it removed Zach from the suspect list, she didn't have a choice. "Someone from MMU, I think. Maybe Alastair Matthews? I know for certain he's taking calls from the Noe family. He had a heated conversation earlier with one of her family members."

Jasper scribbled something down in his notebook. "Thank you. Your reputation for meddling in murder investigations is well known in the area. So, I know sharing information was hard for you."

Xandie rolled her eyes. "I don't go trawling for cadavers. The bodies find me." She pointed to the detective's bright red notebook. "I thought a big city cop would never consider going old school pen and paper."

Jasper smiled wryly. "Electricity mage. Certain electronics hate me." He raised his hands, and a little blue arc wreathed his hand.

Extending a finger, Xandie gently touched the blue light and watched as it petered out when she made contact. No pain, thanks to her Library immunity. The Detective's powers made Braun and Scott's history even more interesting. "If you're an electricity mage, you could have zapped Zach whenever you wanted. Why let him hit you?"

"You *are* quick, aren't you?" Without waiting for her to reply, he continued, "I could have zapped him and laid Zach out senseless. But I didn't. He was my friend. We were as close as brothers. I guess he didn't feel the same way. And maybe I felt guilty too."

Bingo. He'd been seeing Selena behind Braun's back. Conflict of interest much?

"You broke the bro code, didn't you?"

Jasper grimaced. "None of this is your business. But I'm telling you so you understand that he's dangerous. Yes, I dated Selena secretly. She told me she feared Braun finding out. Scared of what he'd do. Apparently, he'd been getting progressively more moody and controlling. And she was right—when he found out, he lost it. We fought, and I ended up in hospital."

"Ever think Selena lied? Or that her powers did a number on him? Trust me, I've met her. Within five minutes, I knew she was a conniving, narcissistic, manipulative, cold fish."

"That's why I'm here. I'm making sure justice is done." He tapped his notebook. "Can I get back to my interview?"

Someone wanted a subject change. "Go for it."

"What's your relationship to Miranda Harrow?"

Wow, that came out of the blue. Her mom? What was the detective doing digging in Miranda Harrow's past? "You know she's my mother. So, why ask me about the relationship?"

"There are open cases concerning both Miranda and Elspeth Harrow. Although some information's classified, there's enough to suggest both women are more than capable of removing obstacles from a loved one's life."

"Obstacles like an ex-girlfriend?"

Jasper nodded.

Xandie leaned over the counter and practiced her own version of an Elspeth cackle. Sadly, lights didn't flicker off and on. Elspeth couldn't care less about Braun's ex-girlfriend, and her mom may care, but she'd have taken Selena down with her Glock. Xandie controlled her braying laughter. She sucked in a quivering breath as she wiped the tears away. Poor Jasper looked frustrated at her reaction.

"Sorry, detective. But if my family committed murder, you wouldn't find a body or any evidence." Xandie smiled widely. "Not that we are or have ever been involved in nefarious wrongdoings resulting in permanent bodily harm."

"Hell, no. She won't go." Elspeth burst into the bakery kitchen with Colin and Theo in tow, along with a sheepish Holly.

"Sorry. Elspeth flipped when she heard the fuzz had cornered you. I couldn't stop her."

Elspeth brandished a hipflask at the detective. "No one takes a Harrow down. Prepare to meet your doom, copper."

She flung her arm back as if preparing to throw her Witchshine-filled hipflask at the detective.

"You get him, doll. I'm prepped and ready to fire." Colin waddled toward Jasper and spun, raising his tush.

Theo raced up to Jasper with Horatio in a saddle on his back. The imp, clothed in a canary yellow jogging suit, with his name bedazzled on the back, raised his tiny sword high and jabbed the mage's ankles.

Xandie backed out of range and covered her eyes. Whatever happened next had nothing to do with her.

Scott moved his legs away from the imp. "Look, she's not being arrested. It's just questions..."

"Arrested?" Elspeth shrieked and threw her flask, hitting Jasper in the middle of his chest.

"Oh, no," Holly wailed and leapt forward to grab Colin but was too late.

"Tally-ho." Colin shuddered, then sagged, a satisfied smirk plastered across his snout.

Xandie gagged as a throat-burning stench flooded the kitchen. Lila's sweet buns that sat proving on the bench collapsed.

Jasper reared up as Horatio stabbed deep with his tooth-pick-sized sword. He covered his nose with his hand as the tuna-scented stench wafted over him.

Holly raced over to the detective and shoved Theo and Horatio away but accidentally clipped Jasper on the head. The detective reared back and bumped into Holly, and the duo went down in a muddle of arms and legs.

"And that's how a Harrow deals with the fuzz, with extreme prejudice and flatulence." Elspeth cackled, and the lights overhead fizzled until they burst with a pop, showering the kitchen with bulb fragments.

Honestly, after this, Xandie expected her entire family to be arrested and incarcerated for the near future.

The bakery door swung open and the two deputies bolted in, handcuffs swinging, as they took in their now unconscious boss. The same detective who had a contrite Holly sitting on top of him.

This day couldn't get any worse.

"I've been working on the chain gang." Elspeth sang off-key and rattled a tin cup against the bars of the jail cell.

"First, that isn't how the song goes, and second, you sound worse than your oversexed crime against nature," Theo yowled at Elspeth and tried to claw her through the bars of his cat cage.

Stopping her singing to glare at the cat, Elspeth slowly extended her finger. "Pull my finger, feline. I dare you."

Shuddering, Xandie slipped between the warring factions of her family. "That's disgusting, Elspeth. We have enough issues with Colin and his bodily functions, let alone yours."

Elspeth sniffed, offense in every line of her body. "Don't descend to the gutter, Library Girl." She flicked the finger out, and a tiny pink arc of electricity zipped along her fuchsia-colored nail. "Static electricity hex nail polish. Would have made the feline's fur stand on end."

Colin rolled on the floor, groaning. "That tuna hex you fed me really doesn't agree with my sensitive system."

Holly draped a blanket over Colin's body, then danced away. "Hopefully, the blanket will contain the fallout."

Family. Can't live with them... And you really can't be interviewed by the police while they're around. "Thanks for the save and all. But he was only asking questions. He hates us now."

"Lila rang us, panicked. We couldn't hear much over the noise of the bakery. We came prepared, or at least Elspeth did." Holly glared at her grandmother. "Aggie had to revive him with smelling salts."

Elspeth shrugged. "He's a big boy. Now he knows not to meddle in the Harrows' business."

"I'll bring backup when I arrest you eventually." Detective Jasper Scott, with a small bandage on his forehead, stood in the unlocked jail cell doorway. "The cell was never locked. You could have left two hours ago."

"I'll leave when I'm good and ready, young man. And if Agatha Braun was here, she'd be ashamed of your conduct." Elspeth hoisted a blanket-covered Colin up and stomped out.

Holly grabbed Theo and Horatio's cage. She winced as she drew level with the detective. "Sorry. So, so, sorry." She dropped her head and scuttled after her grandmother.

Jasper leaned against the wall opposite the jail cell. "After you, Ms. Meyers."

Xandie paused as she drew level with the man. "My family means well. But their execution sucks."

He stifled a weary chuckle. "Actually, I get it. Your family cares and wants to protect you. But I'm not the person they should worry about."

Xandie rolled her eyes as she brushed past him and out into the bullpen where all the empty desks sat. "Yada, yada. Braun's evil. I get it."

"They won't have to worry about Braun for much longer. It's the Noe family you should avoid. They have a dangerous reputation and a thirst for revenge."

Great, another enemy to add to her list. Then Jasper's

words registered. "Why don't I have to worry about Braun? Have you given in and are heading home?"

"I'll be home soon enough. But so will Braun. I have a warrant for his arrest. You need to tell him to come quietly so we can get this trouble sorted quickly."

"What?" Xandie yelled, her screech rivaling Theo's. "He didn't do it. You need to listen to me."

Jasper rubbed his head and winced in pain. "I'm sorry. But his prints came back on those threatening letters you found in the victim's room at the inn. I don't have a choice, Ms. Meyers."

Xandie slapped a hand on the desk in front of her. "You say you don't have a choice? Well, you definitely have an axe to grind. Step carefully, Detective. You don't want the Harrows or the Brauns as enemies." She spun around and followed her family outside. So much for changing his mind. They didn't have a choice anymore. She needed to get to Braun pronto before her annoyingly cute, schedule-challenged shifter ended up in his own jail cell.

Always a drama in Point Muse.

TEN

"Remind me again, why am I agreeing to this?" Zach Braun drained his coffee mug and rinsed it out, staring at the arrayed Harrow women, all with arms folded, all glaring at him.

"Well, dear." Winifred smiled sweetly at the tired looking shifter. "We promised your mother we'd help, and she bargained a favor for our aid. We can't break a spit promise. Imagine the repercussions." Winifred grabbed a saltshaker and sprinkled a pinch over each shoulder.

Elspeth rolled her eyes. "She's an idiot, but she's right this time. Trust us or I'll hex you."

"She's right, kid. You're being railroaded. Take an old dog's advice. Listen to my witch. She knows her stuff."

Poor Braun. He looked like he'd been run over by Lila's bakery van. Dark circles rimmed his eyes, and for the first time since she'd known him, he even sported stubble. "As much as it pains me to agree with my family, you need to stay off the cop's radar until we can dig up solid evidence on another suspect. Mom and Buchanan are still out of town trying to dig up dirt on the Noe family, but they'll contact us as soon as they've got something. Until then, lie low. And Harrow House is as good a place as any to do that. Even more so since the house can defend herself."

Generations of Harrow women had lived, loved, and spelled in the old Victorian-style house. Over the years, the building had grown a personality and soul. If Harrow House didn't want you visiting, you stayed on the porch. If the house needed to contain someone inside, it moved walls around to trap you. And in Braun's case, the house could definitely hide one crotchety bear shifter.

"I'm on record, this is a bad idea. Harrow meddling never ends well." Amelia Harrow, Elspeth's middle daughter and Lila's mother, crossed her arms over her non-existent chest. "Mother is mayhem incarnate. Following her plan is a recipe for disaster."

"Do-gooder," Elspeth muttered under her breath and gave her daughter the stink eye.

"What was that, Mother?" Amelia arched an eyebrow. "Are you telling me this plan won't end in trouble for all involved?"

"Oh, that's definitely going to happen, sourpuss." Colin trotted over to Amelia and lifted his back leg a few inches off the ground.

Amelia growled. "Use it and lose it, pug."

"Everyone but my witchy goddess, Elspeth, is a killjoy." Colin stuck his nose in the air and trotted over to the Harrow matriarch.

She clapped her hands. "It's all decided then. Zachy boy is a treasured houseguest we're protecting. Got it, House?"

A creak and a groan of timbers around them was the only verbal agreement the house could give. Xandie rubbed a door frame. "Thanks, House." It didn't hurt to have some manners when one dealt with sentient buildings.

"So, I hole up in Harrow House while you all investigate?" Braun leaned on the kitchen counter. "You and I both know you'll end up in trouble. I should just turn myself in. Let Jasper deal with the investigation."

"Not happening. Elspeth and Aunt Winifred are right. We made a promise to your mother, and unless you want to deal with them, suck it up."

Lila bolted into the kitchen, almost knocking Holly to the floor. "Decide what you're doing because we have law enforcement company."

Elspeth spun into a whirlwind of action. "Xandie, you and Colin take Zach upstairs to my room. Colin knows what to do. The rest of you make normal as much as you can." She draped herself over a dining room chair. "Lila, you're the greeter. When I give the signal, let the fuzz in."

Xandie huffed at the dramatics but dragged Braun with her as they followed Colin upstairs.

"Why do I feel like she's enjoying this?"

"Because you aren't stupid?" Elspeth lived for mayhem, and the police raiding Harrow House qualified as a top-notch chaos event.

"Right, get your tush in." Colin nudged the door open to Elspeth's room.

Xandie stepped inside, curious. Elspeth's bedroom, like her crafting and creating lair, was forbidden. No entrance, unless allowed. This was the first time she'd even set foot in the room. Wigs in all shades of neon, eye-gouging colors, adorned every available surface. Old-fashioned pictures graced the wall. Including a large one over the bed of a young scowling Elspeth and an elegantly clad, tall, curly-haired man, with laughing brown eyes.

"That must be your grandfather, Lucas." Braun nodded at the picture. "You look a little like him. The same jawline."

"Elspeth would hex you if she heard you say that. She hates the fact we all inherited do-gooder genes from him."

Colin snorted. "She fakes a good game, but she's proud of all of you."

"Have you sniffed some of those dodgy herbs Elspeth has out back?" Elspeth wasn't the kisses and hugs kind of grandmother. She was more a hex your underwear drawer shut and curse the washing machine so it ate your clothing kind of witch.

"She likes to talk at night." Colin shrugged and then hit the wardrobe door with his little pug nose. "Now get moving. That G-Man will be here before I can get you hidden."

"You want me to hide in her closet? No offense, but it doesn't look like it will fit me." Braun flexed his arm muscles.

The slam of a car door distracted Xandie from the movement of bear shifter muscles. Peering outside, she ducked as Jasper Scott stared up at Harrow House. "Right, he's here. Get in the closet now."

Braun opened the closet door, and Colin crowded in next to him. "This wardrobe isn't big enough. I can't even close the door."

"Please, where do you think that writer guy got the idea about a wardrobe that's bigger on the inside? Just move back."

Shuffling, Braun grimaced. "Feels like something wet's trickling down my neck."

Colin shrugged. "Probably Albert."

"Albert?" Xandie had never heard of someone naming a wardrobe, let alone one that leaked.

"Her baby Griffin. She won it in a poker game."

Twin large red eyes blinked in the shadows behind Braun. "It's a baby. What harm can it do? Now hush, he's on the front porch." Xandie slammed the wardrobe door shut on Braun mid-bellow.

"Elspeth would make a killing as a sound proofer." Just in case anyone quizzed what she was doing upstairs, Xandie grabbed an iridescent, rainbow colored wig and trotted downstairs.

"I repeat. You're harboring Zachary Braun in Harrow House. I have a warrant for his arrest. Please turn him over immediately."

Xandie poked her head into the kitchen. Jasper Scott and one of his men stood in the middle of the scowling group of Harrow women. Another deputy was stationed on the front porch. And she'd bet her last dollar a few more were out back, in case Braun went running. Taking a deep breath, Xandie stepped into the kitchen, waving the wig like a surrender flag. "Here you go, Elspeth. Although I don't know why you want a second one when you have that horrible pink one on already."

As everyone spun to stare, Xandie stepped back. "Whoa. Throttle the death stares back. I was only upstairs for a few minutes."

Elspeth sniffed dramatically and stepped away from the law enforcement versus Harrow women standoff. "About time. I thought you got lost up there."

"Colin had a tummy emergency. I think he got into the tuna again this morning."

Amelia shuddered. "That menace of a dog. I've told you

so many times. No tuna. He has a delicately balanced stomach. Seafood disturbs it."

"You're a worrywart." Elspeth waggled a finger at her daughter. "You might be a vet and an animal empath, but I'm the boss in this house. Got it?"

"Honestly, why do I try?" Amelia stomped past Xandie, giving her a wink.

Elspeth yanked the wig out of Xandie's hand. "You better not have touched anything else in my bedroom. I have hex traps everywhere."

"Do I look crazy?"

Jasper cleared his throat to get everyone's attention.

"I have a potion that will deal with that frog throat for you." Winifred skittered away and pulled an emerald-green bottle out of the cupboard. "You need to get onto throat problems quickly." She uncorked the bottle and thrust it at the detective.

Jasper covered his mouth with his free hand and shook his head emphatically.

"Just give in. Trust me, she'll nag you until you do. Besides, it could be serious." Holly nodded sagely and crowded close to the policeman, trying to peer up into his throat.

The detective took a step away and then bellowed, "I do not have a sore throat! I want your attention, and I want Braun delivered immediately into my custody."

"Is that all?" Xandie hopped onto a barstool next to the kitchen bench. She waved a hand at the frazzled police officer. "Look, Detective Scott, we know that Zach didn't kill his ex. We trust and support him, but we aren't keeping him from you. Have a look around the house. You find him, you keep him." Xandie nodded to Elspeth. "As long as the matriarch of the clan commands it, the House won't bite you."

"Ms. Harrow?" The detective spun and faced Elspeth, his large frame tense.

"Whatever." Elspeth waved him away. "Look. But I'm bored. Family get-togethers suck the life out of me."

"I think it's the other way around. Elspeth drains the life out of all of us. I still say she feasts on the life energy of pure virgins."

"Watch what you say, Lila Marie Harrow. Remember that boil I gave the tip of your nose just before homecoming? Care for a repeat?"

"Nope. No. Not me. I said nothing." Lila whispered to Xandie, "It was horrific. Mount Vesuvius of boils. On. My. Nose."

"What did you do?"

"I may have siphoned off some of her Witchshine and sold it to the seniors at school. Made enough to get Maude to witch me up an amazing dress." She risked a glance over her shoulder at Jasper as he and another officer opened doors and cupboards, searching for Braun. "But stealing *and* getting caught is not so good. Elspeth rule. If you can get away with it, then you're consequence free."

"Getting caught is bad, *very* bad," Holly agreed. She joined her cousins. "We all good here?" She raised an eyebrow and waggled it at Xandie.

"We're fine. Colin's upstairs dealing with his complainer... I mean his stomach complaint."

As long as Jasper was busy looking for a disappeared Braun, she could get down to sleuthing. Xandie needed answers, and she needed them fast.

Or her first date would be her last.

ELEVEN

"Won't they kick us out? We aren't supporters or contributors," Xandie whispered to Lila as they entered the conference room.

"The more bodies they have, the more suckers they can get to donate." Lila pointed to two empty chairs at the back of the room. "Head there, so at least we're close to the back if we need to make a quick getaway."

Using her elbows, Xandie mowed a path across to the seats Lila had indicated. "Isn't this a fire hazard? So many people squeezed into one room?"

Lila scooted in next to Xandie. "That's why they moved the meeting from Point Muse Academy hall to the conference room at Point Muse Springs Resort. Plus, with Braun in hiding, and the fire chief out of town, no one is here to care."

Poor bear shifter. The look on his face when Xandie had released him and Colin from the wardrobe yesterday had been priceless. Both the shifter and the pug had worn a covering of silver goo. In other words, baby griffin drool. Apparently, Albert was teething. Not an issue normally, but when you had the body of a lion and the wings of an eagle, the amount of saliva you generated daily could fill a small wading pool. "Any sign of Jasper yet?"

"Not yet. But I'm sure that nosy po-po isn't far away. He probably figures we'll lead him to Braun."

"Not if Elspeth has anything to do with it. Apparently, she has professional pride on the line. Whatever that means."

Scanning the room, Lila nudged Xandie and pointed to the podium where Alastair Matthews stood, whispering with an employee. "Means she's bored and looking for mayhem."

Xandie pretended to glance around the room casually. The good old politician looked a tad discombobulated as he whispered fiercely to his aide. "That looks intense. Don't you think?"

"My husband's upset. Some of our contributors are making noises about withdrawing support. They're concerned about the rumors." Emma Matthews stood beside Xandie's chair, a hand tightly clenched on the back of it.

Matthews' wife looked stunning in a pale suit, her raven-black hair perfectly coiffed, and that same blank gaze on her face. What wasn't normal was the slightly frantic look of panic that flickered for a moment across her face.

"Are you okay?"

Emma blew a breath out and relaxed her death grip on Xandie's chair. "Sorry, I don't do well with crowds. I'm better outside."

Xandie reached into a bag and dragged out a packet of papers. "The Library had this waiting for me when I got back. It's additional information on oak tree and dryad propagation. An update on the information you received earlier."

Life flared in Emma's eyes, and the panic dissipated in a heartbeat. "Thank you so much." She carefully took the papers and hugged them to her chest. "Once I escape the campaign trail, I can get started straight away."

"You don't enjoy campaigning?" Being surrounded constantly by political groupies must get old quickly.

Emma smiled slightly at Xandie's words. "I'm a homebody. A nature lover. Alastair prefers the limelight and normally handles all the political side of things himself. But campaigning for a position on the Supernatural Council is important. So, here I am. Hopefully, not for much longer."

Lila nodded. "I heard the Council brought the vote forward for the empty position."

"We have a week. Alastair and George have moved their campaign timetable up. The murder has upset people."

"Selena Noe. The siren. Her family's a big contributor to MMU."

Emma wrinkled her nose. "The Noes like to manipulate. Control everything. Alistair has a history with them, so he's willing to go along with whatever they want."

Xandie didn't want to upset Emma, but she had to ask. "And Selena? Where does she factor into MMU?"

"She also did what her family told her to." Emma forced a smile. "She was the messenger. Selena passed information onto my husband or his aide, George. There were a lot of meetings. Now, if you'll excuse me, the rally is about to start." With a muted smile, she wandered aimlessly toward her husband.

"Oh, she knows about the affair. Did you see how wooden she got when I mentioned Selena?"

Lila snorted. "She's part dryad. Wood is her favorite medium. But I get what you mean. Do you think she's capable of killing a love rival?"

"Honestly? No." Xandie shook her head. "If it involved a damaged tree, I could see her taking revenge, but her husband's girlfriend? It doesn't fit."

"If everyone can take a seat, we'll get started." George Perse stepped away from the podium, and Alastair Matthews took his place.

"I want to thank all of our supporters and contributors for coming forward and filling this conference space with your support and well-wishes."

Xandie settled back into her chair and let Matthews' voice roll over her. He was using his charisma gift as everyone around her seemed transfixed. Except Lila, who was picking her nails. Harrow blood must provide some kind of barrier against Matthews' gift like the Library did. A stray figure scuttling in caught Xandie's attention. *Polly Harper?* Selena's dresser from the Playhouse had just snuck in and lurked at the edges of the room. Why on earth was she here?

"We've called this meeting to address the rumors about our campaign." Alastair paused for a moment, a chiding expression on his face. "Our campaign pledge at MMU has always been family first and honesty. And a genuine need for others to understand how misunderstood those with monster designations truly are." He waited for the clapping to die down before continuing. "The Supernatural Council has brought their elections forward but never fear. Those of us here at MMU are prepared." Alastair raised his fist into the air, and the room exploded into thunderous applause.

Yeah, this guy had the crowd eating out of his

monstrous hand. Just beware of biters. Xandie nudged Lila. "See who's just skulking? Polly Harper, Selena's dresser."

"Why would she be at an MMU meeting?"

"No clue but monitor her." Xandie covered her yawn with a hand. There was too much love and goodwill in this room for her Harrow genes to cope with. Alastair had called for questions, and the adoring rank-and-file were throwing them thick and fast.

"Mr. Matthews, can you tell me if there's anything to the rumor that the murdered siren, Selena Noe, was your mistress?"

And the not so adoring fans.

Xandie twisted to get a better look. It was that nosy reporter from the bakery, Percival Hague.

"He sees blood in the water and is going in for the kill." Lila winked.

Xandie leaned over and whispered in Lila's ear, "You need to stop watching the Discovery Channel."

Matthews said darkly, "I have no clue who's spreading that rumor, but it's a lie. I've been close to the entire Noe family for years."

"A reliable source has stated they have proof you were carrying on an illicit affair under your wife's nose."

Xandie leaned forward, interested in Matthews' answer.

George Perse spoke hurriedly into the politician's ear, then took his place in front of the microphone. "Mr. Matthews has a full schedule and must attend his next meeting. Any more questions, please address them to MMU headquarters." George gestured to a food-laden table at the back of the room. "Refreshments are provided. Please enjoy." George hustled Matthews off the makeshift stage and through a side exit.

"Well, that was short-lived. No one is leaving though."

Lila was right. Everyone was just moving calmly toward the food. "Maybe they're hungry?"

"Cheapskate politician could have hired my bakery," Lila grumped aloud, causing a few people in front of her to glare.

"Actually, they have an outside company cater meetings and rallies while they're in different towns campaigning. They don't want anyone to accuse them of favoring one business over another."

The intrepid newshound, Percival Hague.

"Impressive question-asking skills, Percival."

The reporter executed an elegant bow. "Percy. And I aim to please my readership. Serious questions must be asked of public figures. Politicians need to be held accountable."

"What actions do you think Alastair Matthews needs to be held accountable for?" And who was Percy's source?

"Matthews runs a family first platform while maintaining an affair with a much younger woman from a major contributor's family. A family that already has too much influence over MMU. Matthews needs to own his actions, or my newspaper will do it for him."

"Who's your source?" Lila smiled coquettishly at the reporter.

"I went to school with you, Lila, and lived through the chupacabra infestation at graduation. I know the menace behind your smile. My source is impeccable but will remain anonymous."

Close, but no flirty cigar, Lila. Whoever the source was, they had to be close to the campaign. Maybe the aide, George? "We're just glad someone's asking hard questions for once."

"I could interview Braun, give the public his version of events?" Percival whipped out his notebook and consulted it for a moment. "I have time this afternoon."

Xandie smiled at the eager reporter. "I have no clue where Police Chief Braun is, but I know while he holds the media in respect, he would choose not to comment on an ongoing investigation."

Lila jabbed Xandie in the ribs and inclined her head casually to the side door where Polly Harper was lurking.

"We need to move before the hordes depart and catch us in a pedestrian traffic jam near the food. Keep fighting the good fight, Percy." Xandie pretended to wander off. "Is he following us?"

"He's disappeared back into the crowd, so who knows?"

Lila was right. Percival used reporter skills and let the crowd cover him. But he was a newshound, so who knew what trail he was following? "Ignore him for now. We need to focus on Selena's dresser, Polly. Why is she here?" Lila, taller than Xandie, took the lead and cleared a path through the crowd. The side exit door stood open an inch. Polly had disappeared out the door, but why?

Peeking through the doorway, Lila motioned Xandie to slide through.

Xandie chose not to feel like Lila was using her as cannon fodder to draw fire first. The exit door led to a dimly lit corridor, an outside exit door at one end, and a set of stairs at the other. "No sign of Polly. We have two choices, door or stairs. Any preference?"

"I'll take the stairs. I've been sampling too much of my cooking." Lila headed to the right and the stairs.

"Guess we're splitting up then. This is the point where I'm screaming at the too-stupid-to-live heroine." Xandie sighed but aimed for the outside exit door. In the same move as earlier, she eased the door open and peered out. The coast was clear. Xandie stepped out but was careful not to close the door in case of a rapid withdrawal.

"Selena told me everything, and I have proof."

Xandie just made out Polly's voice. She followed the sound to the edge of the building and snuck a look. The dresser and someone else stood arguing. Xandie could only see Polly's back. The edge of the building hid her companion. She strained to hear more.

"What proof?"

Polly's companion's tone was too low to work out if the speaker was male or female. Xandie mentally cursed but kept eavesdropping.

"Proof of involvement with Selena. And considering MMU's family first policy, that would be pretty damaging, don't you think?"

Xandie reared back as Polly's companion grabbed her. The sound of tussling gnawed at her nerves. If she could just get a look...

"Do you really think I have it on me? Get real," Polly scoffed at her assailant. "Get your pocketbook out, and you can take my proof and pay for my silence. You know where I'll be."

Oops. Xandie bolted back through the exit door and ran into Lila at the bottom of the stairs.

"Let me guess. You found a clue?"

Xandie dragged Lila under the stairs as cover. "Better than a clue. I just heard Polly, the rabid Selena supporter, blackmailing and threatening someone over Matthews' involvement with Selena."

Lila clicked her fingers. "The jewelry in the handkerchief she dropped at the Playhouse. Did you see who she was talking to by any chance?"

"I wish. No, I didn't, worse luck. But we know where she'll be. The Playhouse, waiting breathlessly for her illegal windfall."

The same place they needed to be to catch the person who had the most motive for offing Selena Noe.

TWELVE

"Seriously. My feet are killing me, and I stand for a living." Lila kicked off her shoes and sighed in relief. She propped her feet up on a coffee table in the Harrow House sitting room.

Colin gagged. "When was the last time you deodorized, kid? Let me tell you, personal grooming is important if you want to land a beau."

Elspeth cackled, and a vase on the mantelpiece rattled. "She's a lost cause. We're pinning our hopes on Xandie and Braun."

Xandie sprayed a mouthful of hot tea over Lila's extended legs. "There are no hopes. No pending. Nothing at all."

"Does that mean you found nothing out?" Winifred placed a tray of sandwiches on the coffee table and shoved Lila's feet off the furniture.

Lila gave everyone the stink eye but reached to grab a sandwich, only to have Winifred slap the back of her hand until she released the food.

"Let Xandie update us first, Lila dear."

Lila dumped the sandwich back onto the plate and glared around the room.

"No one approached Polly, Selena's dresser. The problem is, we've no clue when the meeting is."

Winifred raised her hand. "The props man popped into my candle and potion store today looking for candle props. He told me they're having a late-night rehearsal tonight. And he invited me to come along and have a look." She blushed, red spreading over her cheeks.

"Mom has a date, and I have to work with dead bodies tonight. Where is the justice?" Holly, sprawled in a recliner, kicked her legs out like a pouting little girl.

"It's not a date," Winifred spluttered.

"If it quacks like a duck, walks like a duck, it's a duck... Man, I could really go for some poultry right now." Colin licked his paw and settled next to the sandwich platter with unblinking eyes trained on the plate.

"No. I don't want any Harrows involved in a stakeout. Turn me over to Jasper. He'll be fair." Braun lounged against the doorjamb, hair ruffled and hitting the casual button just right with tight jeans and a long-sleeved shirt.

Xandie licked suddenly dry lips. It added a strange dynamic to their already weird relationship. Him, in Harrow House, casually dressed, with no one to arrest. She was unsure how to feel about it. "We don't have a choice." Xandie snaffled a sandwich and munched, swallowing before adding, "To make sure we're covering all bases, we'll send Holly in undercover to MMU. See what you can find."

Holly stopped swinging her leg. "This is because I'm on dead duty tonight and can't join the stakeout, isn't it?"

Lila rescued a sandwich about to fall into Colin's open black hole of a mouth. "Yes. We want to punish you for playing with dead people. It's all we think of."

"Why you…" Holly grabbed a pillow and lobbed it at Lila, but her aim was off, and it collided with Winifred's sandwich platter, upending the food all over the pug.

"Eureka. This is like a foodie's paradise. Food raining down." Colin rolled to his side and shoveled sandwiches in, only stopping to breathe after every few mouthfuls.

"There goes the night then. Some of those were tuna." Winifred sighed and produced a scarf and tied it around her nose and mouth like a floral mask.

Elspeth tapped the floor with a cane fashioned like a witch's broom. "Focus on the topic, Harrows, not the contents of Colin's stomach."

"Elspeth's right. We'll pay for the contents of Colin's stomach later." Xandie pointed to a shame-faced Holly. "You head to campaign headquarters tomorrow and see what you can find. Lila can prepare a selection of late-night snacks for the actors, and Winifred and I can deliver it and monitor Polly at the same time."

"What about me? I might have a warrant out for my arrest, but I'm used to investigating. Surely I can help somehow?"

"You are. Stay put, and Colin and Elspeth can shifter sit. Run through scenarios and suspect ideas with each other. We'll fill you in if we find anything when we get home. Now… *Break.*" Xandie clapped her hands, and the Harrows darted everywhere.

Braun scowled at Xandie and wandered off, muttering to himself.

"You'll have to speak to him sometime." Elspeth raised an eyebrow. "He's living in Harrow House with most of your relatives."

Xandie ran her hand through her shoulder-length brown hair. "I have spoken to him, but he has that do-good attitude you hate. He wants to turn himself in and let his nemesis do whatever." She liked Zach, more than she wanted to admit, but having him here in Harrow House—she felt bombarded by everyone's expectations, including her own. For the moment, their date and whatever relationship they had was on the back burner until Braun's name was cleared.

"He's a shifter and a police officer. He wants to do the right thing. As much as it makes me sick." Elspeth pretended to spit on the floor, like she had an unpleasant taste in her mouth. "My point is, in my experience, good guys internalizing get moody. Lash out and do something crazy when you least expect it. At least with Harrows, you can expect crazy twenty-four-seven."

"He'll be fine. We just have to prove without any doubt that someone else murdered that home wrecker."

"I hope so. For your sake."

As an ominous warning, that is impressive.

"This is so exciting. Undercover on the mission. Miranda will be so jealous." Winifred clapped her hands like an excited little girl.

"I'm sure Mom won't care. She and Buchanan are on their own mission. They're due back in the next few days, anyway." Xandie adjusted the three containers of food Lila had donated to the keep-Braun-free project. Cookies, cakes, and savory snacks as a bribe to the Playhouse actors. It gave Winifred and Xandie a reason to be at the rehearsal.

A small man, who came up to Xandie's shoulder and had a tidy gray beard, grabbed two lilac-flavored cupcakes. Lila had infused all her cooking for the Playhouse with her

Harrow good vibrations and an inducement spell to share their secrets. Xandie and her aunt had their own stash of non-influenced baked goods to nibble on. The last thing they needed to do was share their plans to catch a killer... *with the killer.*

"Nice to see you, Winifred." The small man took a nibble of his cake and nodded. "Glad you took up my offer for a tour. This old theater needed some brightening up." The man looked at the cupcakes with a frown, then shrugged and continued to munch.

"Oh, Ernie. You say the sweetest things." Winifred giggled, then sobered and drew Xandie forward. "This is my niece, Xandie. She came to help me. She just loves the theater. Xandie, this is Ernie Vast, the props director."

"And she's the Librarian. And the main squeeze of the prime murder suspect in the death of that nasty piece of work siren."

Wow, Lila's witchy baking gifts are epic. "I take it you didn't like Selena much."

"I wouldn't spit on her if she'd been on fire." Ernie crumbled his cake in his fist before realizing what he'd done. He fastidiously brushed the crumbs away. "She was no good and lived for the drama."

"Of the stage?"

"Of hurting people. Anyway she could. Most of the Noe family's like that. She tried to get me fired." He thumped his heavily muscled chest. "Me. This Playhouse couldn't function without my skills with manipulating metal."

"Ernie's a dwarf and can work wonders with metal." Winifred fingered a small silver filigree pin attached to the collar of her shirt. A dainty metal witch on a broomstick.

"This is one of his pieces. He's amazing." She patted the dwarf's now bright red cheek.

"I do my best. I've made all the props here. But that Selena hated it all. Called it provincial." He snorted.

"You didn't like her very much." Maybe another suspect?

"I hated her, but I wasn't the only one." He jerked his head at the couple on the stage. "The understudy and the leading man had a thing until Selena broke them up. Emily's a good girl, but that Cornelius is a dingbat. The other guy standing in the wings yelling at them is the director. He had a thing with that siren years ago, but she dumped him and tried to go back to some cop ex-boyfriend."

Was that cop Braun or Jasper? Her suspect list was growing out of control. The big question was why the cops hadn't found this pool of Selena hatred in the acting community "Who do you think killed Selena?"

The dwarf snorted. "Could be anyone. That girl upset a lot of people, including your own family." Ernie dusted crumbs off his beard and grabbed Winifred's hand. "Ready for your tour?"

Giggling, Winifred waved to Xandie with her free hand. "Make sure Lila's containers don't go on walkies. She gets plastic container rage when they disappear." Winifred took a quick look around, then gave Xandie an exaggerated wink before the props director escorted her on the tour.

Subterfuge was not Aunt Winifred's middle name. Xandie shuffled the food around. Talk about emotional quicksand. She had no choice but to find the killer or Braun would end up in jail. And Xandie would never forgive herself if that happened.

"You're like the bad penny, aren't you? Every time I

turn around, you're there, watching." Polly Harper, Selena's dresser, stood scowling in front of Lila's snack table.

"Actually, my cousin, Lila, offered food for the rehearsal since my Aunt Winifred is getting a tour from the props director. I'm just a body, handling the food. Nothing else." Xandie shrugged. "But if you aren't hungry…" Xandie shifted a container of *tell-me-the truth* cupcakes out of her way.

"I didn't say that." Polly snatched up a pink cupcake and nibbled on a sugar flower. "Your aunt and Ernie are dating?"

"He needed candles for a prop, and my Aunt Winifred helped, so he offered her a tour."

"Ernie's okay. He can get grumpy if you touch his props, and he hated Selena."

"Why?" Come on, witchy cupcake. Work your magic.

"She couldn't stand his work. She tried to get her cousin appointed props director, but Jules has worked with Ernie for years, and he wouldn't do anything Selena wanted, anyway." Polly frowned as she munched on the cake.

"I thought the director and Selena were old friends?"

Polly inhaled and thumped her chest as a piece of cupcake caught in her throat. "They've known each other for a long time, but they weren't close. She had other interests."

"Like MMU? I was at that meeting earlier and saw you there."

Polly dropped her cupcake to the floor and ground it with her foot. "I have no clue what you're talking about. I know nothing about MMU." She turned her back on Xandie and stomped off backstage.

"That wore off quickly."

Xandie squealed and spun around, a hand on her racing

heart. An older blond man with pink racing stripes on the side of his head stood expectantly behind the table.

"Sorry to scare you. I'm Jules, the director."

"Oh, I'm Xandie Meyers." Xandie shook the man's hand and then cocked her head. "What wore off so quickly?"

"The truth spell laid over the cupcakes. Sneaky, but effective. I probably should object to such nefarious actions. Did you find out anything interesting?"

"Define interesting? Why are you upset about me interviewing your employees?"

"I'm not upset. You're the Librarian. You want to solve Selena's murder, go for it. But please excuse me if I decide not to partake in your honesty inducing foods."

"Don't want to spill your secrets?"

Jules chortled. "My past is an open book. To answer your unasked questions—Yes, I have dated Selena. Yes, she left me for someone else. Yes, I couldn't stand her afterward. But no, I didn't kill her. No matter her personality, she was a talented actress and singer. That cover everything?"

"One more. Who do you think killed Selena?"

"Someone who hated her, or maybe equal parts loved her. There's a fine line between love and hate as they say." Jules winked at Xandie and turned to leave, before pausing a moment. "The theater has many layers, both public and private. Seething jealousy, unrequited love, professional competition, and love triangles. The acting world has it all. But Selena and her family take drama to another level. So be careful." With a nod, he disappeared backstage.

"Everyone's a suspect." Xandie stared at the squabbling understudy, Emily, and ex-boyfriend, Cornelius. Everyone here had a motive. Alastair Matthews and his wife had a motive. Even Braun, if she was honest, had a motive. But who was the actual killer?

A bloodcurdling scream, combined with the metallic bang of something large hitting the floor, echoed through the theater. Xandie took off backstage. Her Aunt Winifred was touring with Ernie, how bad could Harrow luck be? She slammed to a stop in front of a crumpled figure with a metal moon covering the top half of the body. The obviously lifeless and blood-covered body.

Winifred stood looking down, a blank expression on her face, Ernie the dwarf next to her, hugging her tight. Winifred raised her head. "It's Polly, Selena's dresser."

The killer had claimed a second victim.

"At least Braun was nowhere near this murder. One less thing to pin on him."

"We have a big problem." Elspeth raced backstage, her wig lopsided and Colin panting behind her.

Always a plot twist in Point Muse.

THIRTEEN

"What do you mean he's disappeared?" Xandie paced the corner of the Playhouse backstage that wasn't roped off by the police.

"I mean, that dirty shifter took advantage of my good nature and devised a sneak attack." Elspeth folded her arms and glared. Dark shadows gathered around her, covering her like the Grim Reaper's cowl.

"Got past you? Queen of chaos and mayhem?" Xandie couldn't remember the last time someone had bettered her maniacal grandmother.

"Sneaky tactics. He let Albert out of the wardrobe just as Colin was settling in for a nap. Albert hadn't even had dinner yet. So, he chased poor Colin around the house and outside. I had to break them up. When I got back inside, the House informed me the bear shifter had scampered. I didn't think he had a devious streak in him."

Elspeth seemed equal parts embarrassed and impressed. Xandie wouldn't want to be Zachery Braun when Elspeth caught up with him.

"It was horrible, doll-face. I'm wasting away with all this

exercise. A juicy red steak would help my iron levels to recover." Colin squinted at Elspeth and Xandie, to see who would take the bait.

Elspeth crumbled first. "Oh, my poor boy. Of course, you'll have steak. We'll put the meal on that mean shifter's tab."

Xandie rolled her eyes. The amount of sweet baby talk Elspeth smothered that pug in, you'd think he'd have tooth decay.

"Why do I always find you at my crime scene?"

Xandie turned as déjà vu slapped her in the face. Braun said the same thing every time he found her at one of his crime scenes. But this time, the annoyed words came from his law enforcement nemesis.

"I wasn't here when it happened. I was tending the snack table."

"I saw it." Winifred lifted a shaking hand but resolutely stepped forward. "Ernie was showing me his props when Polly stormed up and shouted at him about watching who he talked to. The next thing we know, the moon hit her." Winifred shuddered.

Ernie chimed in. "She wasn't the nicest girl around, but she wasn't as bad as Noe."

"Who did she talk to? Her friends?"

"Selena, mainly." Jules, the director, twitched a shoulder. "I saw her speaking to our understudy, Emily, earlier. But otherwise, she kept to herself."

If Emily and Polly weren't friends, why have a convo? Xandie shuffled farther into the shadows backstage, and her foot scuffed against something metallic. Casually crouching, Xandie pretended to retie her shoelaces as she slid the object into her hand. She had a quick glance, then pocketed the object and stood. An MMU campaign button found a short distance from a murder. Xandie wondered if Emily wasn't the only person the dresser had words with. Had Matthews been the figure talking to Polly outside the MMU conference room? The figure Polly blackmailed? Was this Matthews' answer?

"Anything to add, Ms. Meyers? I'm sure you have a theory?"

Smarmy law enforcement officers were an annoyance unto themselves. Somehow, when Braun mouthed off, it was equal parts annoying and cute. Braun's nemesis was just plain irritating. "I have plenty of theories, and none of them involve Zach Braun. But I'm guessing you're not interested."

The detective added a note to his pad and slipped it into his pocket. "At some stage, you must admit Police Chief Braun's involved."

Xandie scoffed. "What happened to keeping an open mind?"

"A second murder happened." The detective turned to Winifred and Ernie. "Anything else to add?"

The couple shook their heads.

"In that case, this is a crime scene. My deputies will take your statements down at the station." With a nod, he dismissed the witnesses.

As Winifred and Ernie shuffled past Xandie, Ernie grabbed her arm and hissed, "I need to speak with you. In the props room."

Xandie bobbed her head slightly in agreement before looking around for Elspeth and Colin.

Elspeth had been large and in charge, whining, before Jasper turned up. So where was she now? Hopefully, Braun and her grandmother were grown up enough to take care of themselves. For now, Xandie needed to find the props room and gather whatever knowledge Ernie had. She headed toward Selena's dressing room. Just before she reached it, she stopped at a door marked Props. "Please don't let a vengeful killer be lurking behind the door." *Or a spider.* Xandie shuddered but carefully opened the door.

"Hurry. I don't want that nosy cop to hear us, and Winifred's waiting for me." Ernie grabbed Xandie and hauled her inside, closing the door quickly behind her. "I can't keep a pretty lady waiting, so this has to be quick."

Gag. No one wanted to think of their aunt like that. Xandie glanced around the room. It was a relatively big area, crowded with metal shelving and various objects of thespian value. Plastic swords, knives, metal shields, back-drops, clothing, hats, and even the odd mannequin or two. Three ornate wooden wardrobes filled with clothing deco-rated one side of the room. "Actors are pack rats *or* hoarders."

"You have no idea. Most of the stuff travels with us, but those wardrobes and the clothing belong to this Playhouse. They stay here."

Xandie found an old chest and perched on it. "What do you know, Ernie?"

The dwarf paced in front of Xandie, avoiding the piles of props. "What *I* know, I don't want that cop to know. You know?"

Great. A babbling murder witness was the last thing she needed. "Take a deep breath and tell me what you know."

"Right." Ernie closed his eyes and inhaled, then exhaled noisily and opened his eyes. "That moon prop that flattened that girl, Polly? The bolts attached to the metal arm were sheared off."

"Wear and tear?"

"Nope. I swapped out the old bolts yesterday. The

sheared ones were brand new. No way could they have worn out so quickly. Someone cut them deliberately."

"The prop could have gone off at any time. Are you saying Polly wasn't the target, just coincidence?"

Ernie shook his head. "I found this too." He reached into his pocket and drew out a severed, skinny rope.

"What is that?"

"Synthetic rope. Different synthetic fibers braided together. Pretty strong."

"What connection does the rope have to Polly's murder?"

He slapped the rope into Xandie's hand. "It's part of a fly system. We use a system of rope lines, blocks, and counterweights, which help the stage crew move props into the air. It attaches to a batten or a metal arm. The moon attaches to the arm." Ernie pointed at the rope Xandie held. "That's cut, it's too uniform."

"Someone waited for Polly to walk under the prop and cut the rope so the moon would hit and kill her." The same someone who'd organized to meet up with Polly, probably in that exact spot. Someone like Alastair Matthews, if the MMU pin was anything to go by. "Thanks, Ernie. I appreciate the info."

"Just between us. I don't want no police special attention." Ernie tipped an imaginary hat and eased the door open. "Best you wait five minutes, make sure the coast is clear, and then disappear. Got it?" Ernie didn't bother to wait for an answer before vanishing out the door.

"Paranoid much?" Xandie closed the door and checked out the props as she waited out her five minutes. She'd always loved old things like scrolls or costumes. Xandie picked her way to one of the open wardrobes and fingered an ornately embroidered golden sleeve. A loud bang sounded outside the room, and the lights flickered before plunging the props area into a black hole. "Elspeth's dentures." Lila's imaginative curses were rubbing off on her. But honestly, she couldn't imagine anything worse than staring at her grandmother's dentures, except for the pitch black of the props room.

Xandie extended a hand and grabbed a wardrobe door. Using it as a guide, she pulled herself up close to it. Something creaked loud in the silent room. Xandie bit back a squeal of terror. Worst-case scenario, she could wedge herself between two of the wardrobes and pray the killer or the cops didn't find her.

Creaking sounded again, closer this time. Xandie squeezed her eyes shut in an effort to control the nerves jumping in her stomach. Then she wiped her palms on her jeans. The dark was suffocating, collapsing in on her. A breeze fluttered against Xandie's neck, and she shivered. *A breeze?* There should be a solid wall behind her. Most Point Muse buildings were a mixture of wood and stone. The Playhouse was one of the oldest buildings in town, so it was more stone. There shouldn't be a breeze.

Something tickled Xandie's neck. She opened her mouth to scream, but a warm hand covered her mouth gently.

"It's me."

Xandie sagged against a warm, hard, and familiar chest. Zach Braun was a dead bear for scaring her.

"Don't say anything. I'm taking my hand away."

Zach dropped his hand and ghosted along her arm until he tangled his fingers with hers.

Xandie shuffled until she could poke his chest with the other hand. "You're in big trouble, Mr. Bear. You scared the hex out of me." Braun huffed a laugh, and his honey-scented breath brushed Xandie's cheek.

"Sorry, I didn't want you to alert anyone that I was in here."

"Elspeth's on the warpath. You tricked her. She's impressed with your sneakiness, but she *will* avenge her besmirched honor." Xandie felt more than saw his shrug in the pitch black.

"I'll deal with that issue when I see her. I didn't want you in danger. And now we have another body."

"And you're on the scene. You don't have an alibi."

"Can't alibi me when I'm hiding, anyway."

The pair froze as the door to the props room opened again, with an ominous creak.

"Follow me," Braun whispered. He gripped Xandie's hand tight and dragged her farther back between the wardrobes.

"It's tight, but you're smaller than me. You should be fine."

"What's tight?" Xandie winced as Braun grunted and jerked against her for a moment. Then his weight disappeared for a few seconds, as did he. "Braun?" She shoved through a skinny opening into a wider alcove. "I swear, if you're about to punk me with a dead spider or a fake ghost, I'll go Harrow hag on your fur-covered, beary butt."

"Shh. Just hang on." He brushed past Xandie and closed the open partition in the wall. "Now we're alone." Braun's words dropped into a pool of warm silence.

His velvet words caused a shiver, equal parts ominous and exciting, to cascade along Xandie's spine.

I'm shut in a room with the potential murder suspect...

FOURTEEN

"Put the light on, or you'll see a Librarian bring some whoop to your bear bottom."

"Hang on."

Xandie heard a rustle, and a soft light illuminated the tiny, boxlike room. *And* a sheepish-looking Zach Braun.

She glared at the shifter. "There's a killer on the loose and you drag me into a coffin of a room in the pitch dark?"

Zach cleared his throat and shot Xandie a wry grin. "Sorry?"

"You will be." Xandie peered at the small room. It was only large enough to have a rickety bed against one wall and a small table and two spindly chairs in the center. "How did you find this dingy lair?"

Braun pulled out a chair and sank into it with a sigh. His sandy colored hair flopped into his eyes, and he pushed it away with a curse.

"Zach?"

"This used to be a bolt hole for patrons of the theater, dodgy dealings, and assignations, that type of thing."

"Doesn't tell me how you knew about it?" Xandie arched an eyebrow at the now blushing police chief.

"My father, the Chief. He had a callout, and I'd just graduated from the Academy and offered to join him." Braun cleared his throat. "A certain upstanding citizen planned an assignation and unfortunately locked himself and his friend in. He sent up a magic flare, and the Chief had to let him out."

"Which upstanding citizen was that?"

"Point Muse law enforcement is the soul of discretion and will never divulge town secrets." He winked but sobered quickly. "It might be better for everyone if secrets *were* brought to light."

Xandie took a seat at the table. "Like Selena's killer?"

"And her family. Have you asked the Library about the Noe family?"

"Only generally. I planned to ask specifics after I got back from the rehearsal tonight, but if we're stuck in here, that might be tomorrow."

Braun winked again. "Not stuck. There's just a trick to opening the door. It's probably safer if we stay here a while, then head out the other exit." He pointed behind Xandie at the bed.

"You want me to get onto that?" Xandie staged a dramatic gasp. "Why, Zachary Braun, I do declare, what would your mother say about your forward manner?"

"That it's about time." Zach stood and held out his hand to Xandie, waiting patiently for her to take it.

Xandie swallowed a lump that magically appeared at the sight of the bear shifter.

He lowered his hand, his face set like stone. "I was only joking. There's a latch under the bed that opens a panel we can crawl through. Comes out near the other actors' dressing rooms."

"Hey." Xandie grabbed both of Braun's hands and squeezed. "I knew you were joking. I just had a minor bad dating attack of anxiety, that's all."

His smile flickered back to natural and became distinctly more predatory. "In that case..." He drew Xandie closer until every inch of their bodies aligned. "I think this has been a long time coming. In fact, I've been thinking about this since I found you upside down, breaking and entering."

"You mean, when you deliberately let me hang upside down after I was locked out of my new home?"

Braun hovered his lips over Xandie's, his breath fanning her cheeks. "Exactly."

She closed her eyes, just like the damsel she hated in a clichéd romantic movie.

"Seriously? You two had all this time in here and that's all you're actually up to?" Elspeth poked her cobwebbed, neon pink wig head out of a shadowed alcove above the bed.

Colin poked his head in next to Elspeth. "Kid, say it ain't so. After all we've meant to each other."

Xandie and Braun reared away and put their hands behind their backs.

Elspeth cackled until she spat a phlegm of dust onto the bed. "This place's housekeeping skills are worse than mine. The coast is clear. You two coming?"

"Xandie can go before me. I'll take up the rear. Make sure no one can follow us."

"I bet you will, Zachy bear." Elspeth pointed a finger at him. "Don't think I've forgotten your sneaky escape earlier. I've had to feed Colin three dinners, just to make him feel better."

"I can reimburse you," he offered quickly.

"I already put it on your tab, anyway." Elspeth grinned wickedly and then prodded Colin. "Back up, sweet pea. We need to get the children home to bed."

Xandie rolled her eyes. Elspeth took way too much delight in verbally torturing her and Braun. Time to nip it in the bud. She climbed up onto the bed. "Move it, pug. Unless you want to end up as Librarian roadkill." She hoisted herself into the hidden passageway with Braun following closely behind.

Keyword, behind. She would never live this down. A choked noise from behind her confirmed the theory. "If you repeat this to anyone, bear, I will bury you deep in the Library."

"My eyes are closed."

Ignoring Braun's antics, Xandie concentrated on Colin. She could already see light at the end of the tunnel, so to speak.

Elspeth grunted, shoved the passage exit open, and tumbled out.

Xandie grimaced as she became tangled in cobwebs and paused to brush her face clean.

Colin stopped at the exit and shook.

"Colin? You okay?"

"I guess the steak hasn't agreed with me either. Sorry for this."

Xandie reared back. "Don't. You. Dare."

"Kid, when you gotta blow, you gotta." Colin shook again and then jumped out.

Covering her mouth, Xandie gagged. Colin and his flatulence were a menace to the senses.

"Please don't tell me." Braun choked and spluttered behind Xandie.

"Colin. It was Colin, got it?" Xandie shoved herself forward, launched out of the hidden passage and into fresh air. She quickly took gulping breaths and moved out of the way as Braun exploded out behind her.

"That dog has medical issues." Braun's mouth opened and closed like a fish as he gulped in untainted air.

"Tell me something I don't know." Xandie brushed cobwebs from her jeans the best she could. The hidden passage had opened close to where Emily and Cornelius had their dressing rooms. She peered up and down the dimly lit hallway. Pretty much deserted. "This place would make a great haunted house at Halloween."

Elspeth sneered. "It's been done. Our house performs much better than this dump."

Harrow House was warm and welcoming. The Playhouse had a deserted and unloved feel about it. Perfect for scaring people at Halloween. A pool of shadows thickened at the end of the hallway. Shadows that moved. Fiery, imaginary ants scratched the back of Xandie's neck. She peered at the shadows, but Emily's dressing room door flew open and distracted her.

Braun flattened himself against the wall, and Xandie moved in front of him while Colin and Elspeth stepped up to block Emily's view.

"Sorry. I heard noises." Emily lowered a heavy makeup case to the ground next to her feet.

"You gonna make us over, sweetie?" Colin sneezed a few times on Emily's feet.

Making a moue of disgust, Emily shuffled out of the way of Colin's snot fallout. "Something like that." She peered up the hallway at the gathered shadows, frowning.

Had Emily been waiting for someone else? "Sorry, Emily. We're just looking for clues and were squabbling."

"Thank goodness it wasn't the killer looking for more victims." Emily shuddered delicately and shoved a clenched fist into her pocket.

Was she worked up enough to clench a fist, or was she holding something she didn't want anyone seeing? Polly and Emily had whispered together before Selena's dresser had died. Emily said she hated Selena and had no reason to talk to Polly. *Unless...* "It's scary having a killer on the run, isn't it? Two bodies now." Xandie shuddered in horror.

"Surely Polly's death was a prop accident?" Emily's eyes flared wide as she stared at Xandie.

Xandie lowered her voice. "Someone sabotaged the prop and killed Polly on purpose."

Paling, Emily fingered her pocket. "It's a tragedy. All caused by Selena and her manipulations." She grimaced. "I guess I'm benefiting from that tragedy. I've stepped into Selena's part now. The show must go on and all that."

"Was that why you and Polly were chatting earlier? Was she going to be your dresser now that you're doing Selena's part?"

Emily nodded with jerky motions. "Yes. That's what it was about."

And Colin could fly. "Poor Polly. Did she speak to anyone other than you tonight?"

"No. She's kept to herself since Selena died." Emily flashed a perfunctory smile at Xandie. "But if you'll excuse me, I've lines to learn." She stepped back and slammed the dressing room door shut.

Elspeth pointed a finger at the shadow-lurking bear shifter. "Get back to Harrow House, pronto, young man. Or I'll tattletale to your mother and you can deal with her."

Braun stepped away from the wall. "No need for threats, Elspeth. I'll go quietly."

Stepping abreast of Xandie, he nudged her shoulder gently. "We'll pick up our conversation where we were so rudely interrupted later." With a wink, he sauntered off.

"Thank Hecate's loins someone has hormones." Elspeth rolled her eyes. "Now, chop-chop. I've a show on embalming to catch."

"Has she gone yet?" Cornelius, the show's leading man and Emily's ex-boyfriend, poked his head out of his own dressing room.

Xandie waved Colin and Elspeth on. "Emily or my grandmother?"

Cornelius looked shamefaced. "Both, although Ms. Harrow doesn't have a reason to hate me yet."

"Yet is the keyword. Emily's back in her room." Xandie took a chance. "But she seemed worried and distracted."

Cornelius sighed and motioned Xandie into his dressing room. "Sorry about the mess. I'm not the most organized of guys." He swept an armful of clothing off a low-set armchair and dumped the pile on the floor next to it.

"I live on my own. Trust me, I understand." Xandie perched on the ragged edge of the chair. "Is Emily okay?"

"She hates me." Cornelius dropped onto a stool in front of his makeup mirror and picked at a loose thread on his pants.

"No offense, but you dumped her for the leading lady. I'd hate you too."

"It was just business. Emily didn't get that. Selena was boosting my career."

Seriously? Dumping your girlfriend was business? "What did Selena get out of this business transaction?"

"She was dating some guy she needed to keep secret. I was camouflage, but I had to stop seeing Emily. I tried to explain everything, but Em wouldn't listen to me."

"Know the name of the guy Selena was seeing?"

"No clue. She kept him away from the public, but he was important. That's all I know."

Alastair Matthews, please step forward. "Were Polly and Emily close?"

"No way. Polly was in Selena's camp all the way. Emily couldn't stand her."

"Why were they having a whispered meeting just before Polly died?"

Cornelius nibbled on a thumbnail. "She won't tell me anything, but I kinda overheard a little before they realized I was nearby."

"And?" It was like leading a kid by the hand.

"Polly gave Emily something. Too scared to keep it. Thought someone was after her. Honestly, that's all I heard."

Xandie had been right. Emily had something in her hand when she'd opened that door. Maybe, like Polly, she'd arranged to meet someone and trade whatever it was for money. Possibly the jewelry Alastair might have given to Selena? "Who do you think killed Selena and Polly?"

"I've no clue, but I think I'm next." Cornelius swallowed, his Adam's apple bobbing wildly. "I like the racing corns. At first, I was up, but in my last race, I lost big time. I owe the Noe family a lot of money. Cash I don't have."

Xandie sighed. "Don't you think getting more involved with the Noe family may have been a bad idea?"

Cornelius wrung his hands. "I know it was stupid, but Selena said she'd handle everything. Now she's dead and her brother has turned up. I saw him backstage just before Polly died."

Another Noe in the picture. But why would he kill his own sister or Polly? "Was Selena close to her family?"

"I felt that they considered her a loose cannon."

And there was the Noe family's motive. Selena embarrassed them. But was it enough to kill for? Xandie nodded at a worried Cornelius. "Thanks for being so honest. Do you want my advice?"

He nodded eagerly.

"Stay away from the Noe family and gambling. It will be the death of you."

Literally.

FIFTEEN

"I hate sentient Libraries." Xandie covered her mouth with a hand as she opened it wide in a bone cracking yawn.

"Not the Library's fault you had a late night." Theo sniffed around his snoring imp, Horatio.

"I was sleuthing, and how was I to know the Library had an early morning delivery schedule?" Xandie poked her tongue out. She'd been neglecting the Library lately, so Theo had a legitimate gripe. Not that she'd admit that.

"You're a Librarian. Shelve instead of yapping or sleeping," Theo yelled and leaped backward as a dozy Horatio lashed out with his tiny toothpick sword before waking up fully.

Hefting a heavy box of reference books on demigod migration patterns, Xandie grunted and dropped it onto her desk. The Library appointment book fluttered open with a snap.

"Do we have any visitors arriving today?" Xandie bent over the book as a small handwritten note appeared under today's date. "Salvatore Noe, limited access. Waiting room only. Information on traditional siren burial rights. Scheduled at nine a.m. sharp." Looks like she had an up close and personal with the Noe family representative in a few minutes. "Saves me from searching out a Noe family member, I guess."

She turned back to the box of books and swiftly unpacked them. Carrying large armfuls to the shelf, she aligned the books and shelved them in their appropriate alphabetical order. Then she dusted her hands off. Working in a Library was dirty work. Even a sentient one like hers. "Library, since Mr. Noe's turning up soon, can you do me a solid and find his information?"

A trio of gold embossed leather-bound books rattled on the shelf. "Thank you." Xandie blew the Library a kiss, gathered up the armful of books, and headed for the welcome room. She shut the door firmly behind her and heard it lock. The welcome room was as it had been when she'd moved in, except the Library had replaced the broken chair that had been used to kill her lawyer. Now the room sported two metal chairs and a small table. And an olive skinned, dark-haired man in his late twenties.

"Apologies, Librarian. The door was unlocked. I assumed the Library expected me." He bent in a deep bow.

"Salvatore Noe, I presume?" Xandie carefully placed the books on the table and turned to face her guest.

"Sal is fine." He smiled charmingly at Xandie.

"I'm Xandie."

"I've heard good things about the newest Librarian."

I bet you have. Putting on a smile of her own, Xandie indicated the chair in front of her. "Please, take a seat. First, I want to offer my sympathy on the passing of your sister, Selena."

Sal inclined his head. "I see the gossip grapevine works admirably in Point Muse."

"The intelligence community would love the Point Muse gossips."

"Those same gossips mentioned you were dating the current suspect for my sister's murder." Sal's smile dropped away from his face, leaving a hardened shell behind.

"He didn't murder Selena. They had history, but he didn't kill her."

Selena's brother laid his hands flat on the table. "Selena was fractious and manipulative at best and at worst?" He shrugged. "I can see how she would drive someone to maddened emotions. Positive or negative, sirens always induce an all-consuming passion."

"Selena had a secret boyfriend. Not Braun, someone else who had a lot to lose if their relationship was exposed."

"You're talking about Alastair Matthews?"

Xandie gaped. "You knew?"

"We were aware of the relationship. As we are strong supporters of MMU, political ramifications concern the family. But as my sister was an adult, we could only suggest, not force."

"But I've heard forcing is a favorite tool of the Noe family."

"Cornelius Haven." Sal tsked. "Such a creative talent to waste on poor choices and gambling." He leaned forward, took Xandie's hand gently in his own. "Please, believe me, Xandie. We mean no harm to those who owe us a financial debt. Why would we hurt them? We'd never see our financial contributions repaid. But sometimes incentives are required. Nothing dangerous or life harming."

Xandie slid her hand away. This slick siren had an answer for everything. "Aren't you worried the killer is most likely Alastair Matthews? The man you've invested a substantial amount of family time and funds into?"

"The family always gets their pound of flesh. The Library would do well to remember that." Sal stood and tapped the books. "Please thank the Library for its offer of research material, but I've just realized I have all the knowledge that I need." Selena's brother nodded to Xandie before departing.

Why did that feel like a warning?

***

"Remind me why we're doing this again?" Xandie ran the piping bag nozzle carefully around the edge of the violet-colored cupcake.

"We're pledging our support behind MMU. We may not be monsters, although Elspeth probably counts, but some of our best friends *are* shifters." Lila expertly iced five cupcakes to Xandie's messy one.

Biting her lip, Xandie carefully piped a small flower in the middle of the cupcake. "Why do I have to help? You're the baker."

"Your boyfriend is a murder suspect. The rest of us are all just support. Now mush...*err*...ice." Lila poked Xandie in the rib cage and went back to icing. "Besides, I'm giving up my bakery kitchen to do this in the Point Muse Springs Resort kitchens. All open and above board, no poison in the mix." Lila pointed to Emma Matthews, who sat at the end of the kitchen counter, humming and playing with sugared flowers. "We even have a safety observer."

Emma looked up, still humming, and waved to Xandie.

"I don't think she's baking with a full set of measuring cups." Holly moved cupcakes into cardboard cartons.

"She *is* a dryad-human hybrid. That goes without saying." Lila wiped her hands and took away Xandie's mangled cupcake. "This is pitiful. Remind me why I put you on icing duty?"

"You're crazy. That's why." Xandie pointed at her cousin, Holly. "Why didn't she get the icing torture?"

Holly struck a pose. "I am undercover. As a banshee, I qualify as a monster." She looked over her shoulder at Emma. "Should we be saying this in front of her?"

"Unless you're a plant, or look like a plant, or are holding a plant, I don't think Emma is really interested in what you talk about." Lila clapped her hands. "Right, let's get this spying operation on the road."

Emma smiled brightly at the cousins. "I like you three. You make lovely flowers, and the Library gave me wonderful books on planting. If you want to spy on my husband, he's set up an office in a boardroom off the main conference room. He has lots of papers in there." Emma wandered off, shoes still under the kitchen stool she'd perched on.

"Is that normal behavior for dryads?" The woman didn't seem to care much about her husband, only trees and plants.

"They get more aware the closer they are to their trees. I think she's been away from home too long." Holly grabbed a handful of cartons and carefully balanced them. "Hold the door open."

Lila quickly propped the door open so they could all go through without holding it. "It will take a few minutes, but we should be able to get this lot into the conference room with no issues. The Diner and Mayweather Inn are also showcasing their food. There'll be plenty of food to choose from and the Resort offered their own servers. We just have to deliver the grub and enjoy ourselves at the rally." Lila followed Holly out the door with her own armful of cartons.

Sighing, Xandie picked up her pile of boxes and prayed she didn't do her normal, clumsy routine and end up face down in violet-colored cupcakes.

"Can I help?"

Xandie squealed and spun around, her top box teetering.

"Sorry. I thought you heard me." George Perse grabbed Xandie's top box before it toppled. "I just wanted to say thank you for helping to supply the food for the bake sale. Every bit helps when you're fundraising."

Especially when the head of the political party was in deep with the siren mafia. "No worries. Happy to help."

"Point Muse has been so welcoming to MMU. Some towns aren't so open-minded."

"Except for the odd murder or three, Point Muse isn't such a terrible place to live."

George slowed to a stop. "Ms. Noe and Ms. Harper's deaths are tragic and horrible. I truly hope the police can catch the person responsible for them."

"Only one problem with that. The police have the wrong suspect in their sights."

"I've heard that a certain police chief is under suspicion."

"No one believes he did it, except the new police detective, who has an ax to grind."

Matthews' aide nodded sympathetically. "It's hard to see fault in those we love. But sometimes one has to admit their family member or loved one is toxic and move on." An undeniable emotion flitted across his face before it smoothed out to blandness.

"And sometimes someone's framing them." Xandie started walking, and George trotted behind until he'd caught up.

"Sorry. I didn't mean to imply anything about your bear shifter."

Xandie paused in the doorway of the bake sale room. Matthews had set up his office off the conference room that housed the fundraising bake sale. She couldn't see any doors, but there was an alcove off to one side. His office must open off that. She studied the room. Plenty of people were already milling about, and the bake sale hadn't even started. Emma Matthews walked past and waved a vague smile in Xandie's direction. "Is Emma always so..."

"Vacant?" George nodded. "As long as I've been with Mr. Matthews, and that's six months now. In fairness, she's a dryad, or at least partially. The last few months have involved a substantial amount of time away. She's more focused when she's closer to her trees."

"Are she and Mr. Matthews close?"

George shot Xandie a narrowed glance. "They're married. Emma is a supportive wife. She is one hundred percent behind her husband and his policies."

Sure she is. As long as her husband carried out his politicking close to home and her trees. "Of course."

Lila waved Xandie over to a large portable table set up with masses of sweet and savory baked goods. Xandie carefully placed her armload of boxes on the table and Matthews' aide followed suit. Smiling sweetly, she laid a hand on George's arm. "Thanks for the help. Are you hanging around and enjoying the fruits of Lila's labors?"

George patted Xandie's hand and then deftly slid it away. "Mr. Matthews and I have a meeting at Mayweather Inn shortly. Ms. Mayweather kindly offered us a private room. In fact..." He checked his watch. "We should have left already. If you'll excuse me?" The aide quickly vacated the room.

"What did you say? He disappeared really quickly."

"I was all that was warm and welcoming. What's the bet, cousin dear, that the good old politician has a meeting with the Noe family representative?" Xandie wondered just how much pressure the charming Salvatore Noe was bringing to bear on the philandering politician. Had Selena's family called in his marker? Maybe Selena wanted to go public, or threatened to go public, with their affair and he'd snapped. Whatever the reason, Matthews was in it up to his eyeballs.

She just needed to prove it.

SIXTEEN

Xandie reached for a white chocolate and emerald-green cupcake.

Lila slapped her hand. "You touch it, you bought it."

"At least she doesn't have claws." Priss Makepeace, dragon, cousin to Es Penne and friend to the Harrow family, stood grinning at them.

"Priss," Lila squealed and gave the dragon a quick hug. "I thought you were on a secretive dragon expedition?"

Xandie rolled her eyes at Lila's drama llama antics. Priss was a hybrid dragon and was the eldest granddaughter of Marjorie Penne, matriarch of the Pendrakon clan. A while ago, someone framed her friend for the murder of a dodgy-dealing dragon cousin. The Harrows helped clear her name, and Priss joined the ranks of Harrow cronies.

"Grandmother heard about Braun's troubles. She sent for me. Figured an extra minion for Xandie to order around might help."

Xandie gave the blonde, bouncy, and deadly dragon a quick squeeze. Priss was a champion fencer, plus she had large fangs and claws. Perfect if they had to face down a slimy killer politician. "Just in time. How does a little breaking and entering sound to you?"

"Right up my alley. Lead on, Sherlock Librarian." Priss offered an arm to Xandie.

"Lila, are you done unloading goodies?"

"As of now, yes." Lila twitched a cupcake onto a plate and winked at a server standing nearby. "All yours, Phil. Taste, but be wary of the cupcakes with passion flowers on top. They put a zing in your step." She smiled and joined Xandie and Priss. "What's the game plan?"

"Raid Matthews' office for evidence and make sure we don't get caught."

"Crab puff? Free sample from Mayweather Inn's kitchens." A short, dumpy, server with long, curly blond hair sashayed up, chewing gum.

"No, thank you." Xandie stared at the waitress. Something familiar about the woman gnawed on her sleuthing nerve.

"Do yourself a favor. Take a step away from that bakery standard grub and taste elegance." She snapped her gum and winked at Xandie. Winked with an amber-colored eye.

"Why, you nasty..." Lila launched herself at the waitress and her plate.

"Holly? Is that you?" Xandie couldn't believe the sight before her. Her quiet, death-obsessed, slim cousin had transformed into a trashy, dumpy, gum-snapping, mouthy waitress.

"Well, you wanted me undercover. Elspeth had some ideas and here I am."

"You don't really think my food is only standard, do you?" Lila whined, her bottom lip wobbling.

"No, needy baker. Your food is multi-layered and delicious compared to what the four-star chef from

Mayweather Inn produces." She shoved her plate at Lila. "See what you think."

Lila took the puff and a paper napkin mutinously from her cousin and snapped off a savage bite. Her face lit up as she spat it into the napkin and placed it back on the tray. "That's truly horrible. *Huzzah.*" She flung her hands up like a prizefighter and danced a victorious jig.

"Unobtrusive, remember? No attention? Stop dancing," Xandie hissed at Lila. "Holly, we're searching Matthews' office. You linger close and waylay him if he comes back before we finish. Lila, you watch as well and warn us when you see her talking to him. The bathroom's apparently in the same alcove, so we can slip in and pretend we were having a bathroom break."

"You got it, boss." Holly snapped her gum again and weaved off into the crowd.

"I don't think Lila's the only drama llama in your family." Priss bit back a snicker at the look on Lila's face while she watched her cousin's antics.

"Sadly, I think you're right. Lila, prop up the wall. Remember, warn us if you see Holly and Matthews together."

Lila nodded and disappeared.

"Ready to rumble, Makepeace?"

"Whenever you are, Meyers."

The girls linked arms and wandered around the room, casually making their way to Matthews' office.

Little pockets of Point Muse residents gathered in spots around the room. Xandie fought the need to bare her teeth as she passed whispering conversations. She could just imagine what the old biddies were gossiping about.

"Remember our deal?" Rose Mayweather hissed at Xandie as she gathered in close to her.

Rose, descendant of Aphrodite, was resplendent in a pastel pink, nineteen fifties style dress with matching pink flowers in her silvery beehive hairdo. Xandie mentally threw up. Pink was not one of her favorite colors. "The deal where we catch a killer and the respectable Mayweather Inn's name is then out of the investigation. That deal?"

"Yes. Why is it taking so long? People are talking."

"Hasn't it only been a few days?" Priss stared, confused, at the inn owner.

"That's beside the point," Rose growled. "Susie Barnes is sniffing around. Solve this now." Faking a smile, she wandered off, petticoats flaring.

"So much for Aphrodite's descendant. There's no love in that black heart." Xandie tightened her grip on her friend's arm. "We need to search the office, pronto."

"Your wish is my command, sleuthing boss." Priss swung Xandie into the deserted alcove near the bathroom and Matthews' office doorway.

Dropping to her knees, Xandie once again pretended to tie her shoelace. A favorite trick of hers while pretending to be casual. "No one's watching, so let's try the door."

Priss twisted the handle. "It's locked. Good thing I came with my own key though." She flicked out a dragon claw and fiddled with the lock for a few moments. "Open sesame."

Xandie nudged the door open. "I'd rather use your claw than Great-Aunt Rose's skeleton key finger." She slipped into the room, Priss close behind her. Matthews was neat and organized, nothing like Selena. Opposites must attract.

"What are we looking for?"

"Anything with Selena's name on it or the Noe family's. Evidence that clears Braun? The smoking gun?" Xandie smiled weakly. She had no clue what she was looking for. Hopefully, she'd know it when it slapped her in the face.

"Righto." Priss rifled through a filing cabinet.

Taking his desk, Xandie methodically searched one drawer at a time. The only thing of interest she found was a pack of gum. "Anything?"

"Sorry. Not yet."

Sighing, Xandie moved to the bookcase. Sliding a book out, she flicked through the different texts, in case a slippery politician had hidden incriminating evidence between the pages. She kneeled as she reached the bottom two shelves of the heavy wooden bookcase, then picked up a mind-numbing tome on monster rights in the penal system. Upending it, she gave it a quick shake and squealed when a small bound pack of letters fell out. "Eureka. We have something interesting."

Priss quickly joined Xandie as she slid out a letter and skim read it. "These are from Selena. She wasn't happy with Matthews keeping her on the down low."

"The siren wanted the spotlight, not the shadow."

"Exactly." Xandie read aloud, "I'm tired of coming third place behind your campaign and wife. Something has to change." She picked up another. "You promised you would change and put me first. But you haven't." She slid out the third letter. "I've had it. You're going to regret ignoring me. Soon, everyone's going to see my shiny truth, and you're finished." Xandie looked up at Priss, eyes wide. "Sounds like blackmail to me. It gives Matthews motive. But does it get Braun off the hook?"

"It puts Matthews at the top of the suspect list."

Xandie collected the letters and slipped them into her pocket. Something about that line, *my shiny truth*, was itching at her brain. She spotted another piece of paper caught in the book. She pulled it out and opened it. "Looks like Matthews was into the Noe family coffers for an even five hundred grand. No wonder Selena's brother is sniffing around. His family must want him to monitor their investment even if he killed their daughter." Xandie placed the book back on the shelf. "We've got what we came for. Let's get out of here."

Nodding, Priss took the lead. Peering out into the alcove, she motioned Xandie to go first.

Tucking herself against the wall, Xandie peeped out into the crowd. More people had turned up for the bake sale, thankfully, hiding their breaking and entering. She scooted across to the bathroom entrance, then turned and sidled out into the crowd, pretending she'd just been using the bathroom.

"Casually done, just in time." Lila joined Xandie. She nodded to the conference room entrance where Holly had Matthews and his aide held up with a sample tray. "Find anything?"

"Enough to know Selena was blackmailing Matthews and he was in debt to her family for five hundred thousand dollars."

"Sounds promising."

"We need to get out of here, pronto. *Before* he rumbles to the fact I've raided his office." Someone bumped into Xandie's back and sent her flying into Lila's arms.

"I am so sorry, Xandie. It's getting crowded in here." A contrite Emily, Selena's understudy, grimaced. "I didn't think a political bake sale would be so popular."

Xandie righted herself. "It's Point Muse. The only thing more popular than the bake sale is a funeral or a murder." Xandie smiled at the young actress, or she tried to. Emily wouldn't look her in the eyes. In fact, she kept staring over her shoulder at Alastair Matthews and his aide. "Are you okay, Emily?"

Emily forced a smile to her face. "Not really. I'm leaving the Playhouse and Point Muse. The stress of Selena and Polly's deaths are affecting my voice. I'm leaving as soon as I finish talking to you."

Little Emily was doing a bunk. Running away. But why? As far as Xandie was concerned, Emily had nothing to do with the murders. Unless she'd spoken to Polly and now had information that scared her. "What's wrong? Have you been threatened?"

"Not yet. Someone saw me talking to Polly. I'm getting out of here before I end up at the funeral home like they did." Emily surreptitiously grabbed Xandie's hand and dumped something cold into it. "You'll know what to do with this. I'm outta here." Emily turned her back on Xandie and dodged through the crowd.

"What did she give you?" Priss closed ranks beside Xandie, covering her from view. Lila did the same on the other side.

Xandie opened her hand. Emily had given her Selena's bracelet. A shiny, silver bracelet with a few little stones hanging off it and an inscription engraved on the clasp. "A to S. Not exactly romantic."

"That's how she did it." Priss pointed to a pale translucent stone that hung off the bracelet.

"What do you mean?"

"That's a Moonstone. My dad would use them occasionally when he was undercover, stalking dragon prey."

Priss Makepeace was a dragon-human hybrid. Her late mother had been a Pendrakon, but her father, Simon Makepeace, had been a human dragonslayer. "And what does it do?"

"If the right spell is on it, the stone records images and sometimes audio."

Xandie clicked her fingers. "*My shiny truth.* She recorded all their rendezvous. No wonder he wanted to kill her and anyone else who has had that bracelet. It's a record that will bring his political career down."

Lila nodded. "That explains Selena and Polly. But it also means you need to solve the murder and get rid of that bracelet before he comes after you."

"What?"

"You're a target." The three girls' heads snapped up at the unexpected voice. Xandie grimaced. Harrow bad luck always struck at the wrong time.

"Sorry, girls. I was coming over to see how you were doing, and he tagged along." Aggie Braun scowled at her son's nemesis, Detective Jasper Scott.

"Seems like you ignored me when I told you not to investigate."

"You'll get used to it." Xandie closed her fist around the bracelet.

"I think you and I need to have a private discussion, don't you?" He quirked an eyebrow, waiting for her reply.

The jig is up. She had no choice but to agree. Hopefully, he'd hear her out. Otherwise, Braun had no chance to clear his name. And that was something she wouldn't stand for.

Librarian to the rescue.

SEVENTEEN

"You're not under arrest. You didn't need to bring an entourage."

"A Harrow always has backup." Lila glared at the detective.

"Welcome to my world." Xandie rolled her eyes.

"We're here to make sure you don't pull any tricks." Aggie crossed her arms over her chest and flexed her broad bear shifter shoulders.

"Aggie, you know me. Xandie has solid information about the case. I need to know what it is. That's all."

"I know the person you used to be. Not the detective railroading my Zachy bear."

Sadness flickered across Jasper's face for a moment. "All I want to do is see justice served for Selena and Polly Harper."

Aggie slammed a hand down on the Library desk. "It always comes down to that slanderous siren, doesn't it?"

Jasper heaved a sigh and placed his notepad on the seat next to him. "Let's get this out of the way first." He took a breath and stared at Aggie. "I've always regretted how things turned out between Zach, Selena, and me."

"You went behind my boy's back with that monstrous floozy. Your betrayal is worse than hers."

"He ended up in the hospital, so I think he may have paid for his mistake," Holly pointed out fairly.

"What side are you on, Death Girl?" Lila hissed at her cousin.

"Can we just listen to him first before we squabble?"

Jasper nodded his thanks to Xandie. "I'm not proud of my actions. Seeing Selena behind Zach's back is something I'll regret forever. But at the time, it felt like it was my only course of action. I didn't know until much later what Selena had done to both of us. Unfortunately, it was way, way too late and pig-headed Zach refused to talk to me."

"She whammied both of you, didn't she? That's why you went behind his back. And why you fought each other."

"She found some way to amplify her gifts. To an almost murderous level. It was weeks before her influence faded from my system."

"But by then, Zach had graduated and left Point Muse, and Selena had disappeared with her producer," Aggie huffed.

"Exactly. So, I concentrated on my career. When I heard about Selena's murder and Zach's involvement, I spoke to my bosses. They agreed to overlook my history and send me to head the investigation." He focused on Aggie. "I'm not here to railroad anyone. I wanted Zach in custody so I could clear his name. I know he'd never kill anyone for revenge or to protect himself. But he has a temper. You need to know that."

"I was too ashamed to speak to you after I lost control and put you in the hospital." Braun stood highlighted in the afternoon sun pouring into the Library, a satisfied Elspeth and a preening Colin behind him.

Standing, Xandie walked over to the shifter. "She lied to both of you and used her gifts to suck you in and ramp up the obsession and violence. That's not your fault, but Selena sadly didn't learn from her mistakes, and she paid dearly." She led him to the couch and sat next to him, leaning against his warm body.

Colin pranced forward, growling at Theo, Xandie's black feline guardian. "Doll-face decided it's time to let the shifter out for semi-good behavior. I've forgiven him for the baby griffin incident."

Elspeth sniffed and fluffed her turquoise wig which matched her velour jogging suit. "We'll sort out suitable consequences for the incident at a later date." She strode over to Aggie. "Well, old girl. Has time healed old wounds?"

"In this case, an apology and an explanation worked well enough. If Zachy's satisfied, so am I." She gave Jasper a small smile.

He picked up his notebook again. "Can we get back to whatever it is you found that will clear Zach of a murder charge?"

Dumping the threatening letters and the IOU in the middle of the small table, Xandie pointed out, "Selena was blackmailing Matthews to make their affair public, and he was in the hole financially to her family to the tune of five hundred thousand dollars." Xandie held up Selena's bracelet. "Matthews gave her this bracelet. She added a moonstone onto it and recorded them on this hexed stone. Considering his platform on monsters and family first, I don't think his constituents, or the Noe family, would've been happy with him."

Elspeth snatched up the bracelet. "Let's get a gander at

what dirt the siren had. Shame we don't have popcorn." She flicked the stone and uttered a word under her breath. An image without audio flickered into the air above everyone's head, solidifying until it was like a silent movie.

Xandie leaned forward as Braun stiffened. She squinted at the picture until she realized it was Salvatore Noe, Selina's brother, handing money to Mathews. Wads of it. "That almost looks like a bribe from the Noe family to Matthews, doesn't it?"

"And Selena recorded it." Zach grunted. "Neither the politician nor her family would've been happy with recorded proof of the transaction."

The image froze for a moment before forming a new picture. Xandie grimaced. Selena in a clinch with Matthews and George, the aide, lurking in the background as lookout. "Fast forward past the icky bits, please."

"Yeah, it offends my sensitive sensibilities. And no one wants me to get an upset tummy. You know what I mean?" Colin said to the room at large.

Elspeth snapped her fingers, and the image changed again. This time, it showed Selena and Matthews arguing, the aide nowhere in sight. Selena's face was bright red, and she shoved the politician back. He flung his hand in the air and stormed out. Watching from another doorway was Emma Matthews. She'd seen the whole incident.

"His wife knew all about the affair." Lila nodded to the image. "She doesn't exactly look devastated either."

"Get the feeling the only thing she feels passionate about are her trees," Xandie agreed with Lila. The poor dryad just wanted to go home.

The image flickered again to Selena in a dressing room, tearing into a package. Her obvious delight at receiving jewelry sent a chilling shiver down Xandie's spine. "She'd no clue the killer was setting her up to die in your cheeseburger, framing you at the same time."

Jasper cleared his throat. "In case anyone is wondering, I've an alibi for Selena's death."

Elspeth waved the detective's comments away. "You're old news. We're more interested in the home movies."

Another picture, this time with Polly, Selena's dresser, arguing with a shadow-covered man.

"Whoever that is, they're professional. That's a high-grade shadow hex covering him. We won't be able to get any images of his face." Elspeth nodded to the dark figure in front of Polly.

"How can you tell it's a man?" Priss frowned and cocked her head, staring at the image.

"Experience, toots. My girl's got it going on." Colin puffed his chest out proudly.

The shadowed man grabbed Polly's wrist and tightened his fingers. She opened her mouth in an obvious gasp and shook her attacker off. Xandie peered at the background of the picture. "That's backstage at the Playhouse. Near where she died."

"Probably not long before the incident." Braun frowned.

"What's wrong?"

Braun answered Xandie without looking away from the image. "The shadow man. Something's off."

Elspeth flipped her fingers again. "This is the last image saved."

Xandie stiffened. This time it was her and Emily at the MMU bake sale. Emily clandestinely passed the bracelet to Xandie and then disappeared into the crowd. Somehow, the image had swung around and focused on Matthews and his aide, with Holly hovering in the background. Both men were facing toward Xandie. "Did they see Emily hand me the bracelet?"

Jasper leaned forward. "It's not clear, but they *were* facing in the right direction to see you. But possibly with the crowd swirling around, they might not have seen anything."

Braun reached an arm around Xandie's waist. "If they saw, then Xandie's at risk." He turned her to face him. "I think you need to give Jasper the bracelet. He can leak it to the gossips that he has it. That way, you aren't at risk anymore."

How sweet. Braun was trying to protect her. Xandie patted his whiskery cheek. "Or I can keep hold of it, and you can use me as bait to flush Matthews out."

Braun dropped his arm from Xandie's waist, and the room exploded into noise, with everyone talking at once. She held up a hand. "Whoa there, nervous nellies. Not like I haven't done this before. So, why the drama?"

Theo arched his back and hissed at her. "You have a death wish. Let the brawny detective handle it. That's why they pay him the minimum wage."

"It's all about the cold hard cash with you felines, isn't it?" Colin sneered at Theo.

"Why, you dogenstein..." Theo lunged at Colin, but Elspeth separated the animals with a single glare.

"I don't want to risk the Librarian, but MMU doesn't have much longer in town. A few more days at the most. The big political rally is coming up, and that's the last event. I hate to say it, but we need to bring Matthews down before he disappears."

Braun rubbed his forehead and turned to Xandie. "I know you're more than capable of dealing with trouble, but I still don't like putting you purposefully in danger." He rubbed a calloused hand down Xandie's arm. "We still need to finish that first date." He waggled his furry eyebrows at her comically.

Xandie snorted at his antics. This annoying bear shifter had wiggled his way into her affections. As Elspeth would've said, he revved her engine. But she had a job to do and that meant catching a killer.

"*I have a plan...*"

EIGHTEEN

"You said you had a plan?"

"I lied." Xandie winked at Lila. "I just wanted everyone to stop squabbling and leave last night."

"Oh, they did. They left fuming because you wouldn't share your non-existent plan, and Braun left in handcuffs."

"Hey, I had no clue Jasper would do that. Besides, it's Elspeth's fault for hiding him."

Jasper had apologized, but a warrant had been issued, and he'd reasoned with Braun in jail when or if the killer struck again, it would clear Zach's name. But seeing the shifter in spelled cuffs hadn't sat well with anyone. She swallowed the lump that filled her throat at the memory.

"Fine. But you've slept on it now. What's your plan?"

Xandie pointed to the stage. "That's the plan."

"Aunt Winifred is the only plan you came up with? We're doomed." Lila sagged into a chair and groaned.

Xandie tapped Lila on the shoulder with a small fist. "Winifred can sing, and she obviously has the streak of Harrow drama. I mean, look at her."

Winifred stood in the middle of the spotlight that Ernie had turned on her, her arms outstretched as she held a high note. Winifred literally glowed.

Jules hustled up the Playhouse stairs and stopped next to Xandie. "I must admit, I had doubts when you suggested her. She's honestly too old for the role, but her singing and acting are magnificent."

"Who'd figure a Harrow for a ticket-selling drama queen?" Lila giggled until Xandie elbowed her.

"Winifred's talented, and we didn't want the Playhouse to close. You only have a week left before you're supposed to move on, anyway. Why not try her out?"

Jules nodded. "Selena and Polly's murders have delayed our timetable somewhat, but with Winifred, we can at least get some kind of performance up and running for Point Muse. We have holidays coming to us, so it gives us time to find a new leading lady since Emily's also disappeared."

Winifred dropped the note and stepped into her next cue. Cornelius, the leading man, clasped Winifred awkwardly in his arms as she pretended to swoon. He wobbled and they both went down in a jumble of limbs. "I think they need more practice."

"A few kinks. But the show must go on. Kisses." Jules air kissed Xandie and rushed off, bellowing at Winifred and Cornelius.

Lila looked around. "Where's Elspeth? I thought she'd be in the front row heckling Winifred non-stop."

Xandie shot Lila a worried look. "I don't know. Winifred told me she was around Harrow House this morning. And Holly mentioned she'd heard Elspeth muttering and banging in her creation cave."

"The mad scientist lair, you mean."

Her grandmother liked to meddle in mother nature's business. Colin, the talking, farting pug, was proof of that. "Any idea what she's planning?"

Lila shrugged. "Elspeth's a maniacal genius. It could be anything. What are we doing at the Playhouse, other than watching Winifred fall over?"

"We're meeting a consultant who'll help us in our plan to track the killer."

"What poor sap have you sucked into your sleuthing web?"

"Him." Xandie pointed to a skinny figure taking the Playhouse steps two at a time. "Thanks for meeting me here, Percy."

The reporter flopped down on a seat in front of Xandie. "You said stop the presses. So, this better be good. My issue is due to go out tonight."

"How would you like to help me catch a killer and get an exclusive for your next issue?"

Percy whipped out a voice recorder and a notepad. "Tell me more."

"I need you to update your readers unofficially on the investigation of Selena Noe's and Polly Harper's murders."

"And that update would be worth my while?"

"The Harrows would owe you a favor, and you'd help to catch a killer. How does that sound?"

Percy shook Xandie's hand. "Sounds like a deal to me. What do you want me to say?"

The plan was falling into place. Now to bait the hook. "I want you to tell your readers that Police Chief Braun is helping law enforcement with their inquiries."

"In other words, the police arrested him."

Xandie shot Lila a don't-talk glare and then confirmed

Percy's guess. "The police now have a prime suspect in mind, thanks to a tip from a member of the public."

"Hope you got more than that because, so far, I could get that information out of one of my sources."

"The police are following multiple leads, including evidence in the Librarian's possession. The police have also found a connection between the Misunderstood Monsters United party and the traveling Playhouse. And use whatever dramatic reporter language you need to sell the story. But I need you to mention that the Librarian has the evidence. *And* I need it to go out tonight."

Percy nodded. "You got a deal, but I want an exclusive after you take the killer down."

"I've no clue what you're talking about." Xandie tried to look innocent but failed miserably as Lila and Percy cracked up laughing.

Sobering, Percy cleared his throat. "All right. I'll get the issue out within the next few hours. The big MMU rally is on late tomorrow afternoon, so it's good timing. Stay out of trouble until then." Percy winked before taking his leave of the cousins.

"I hope you know what you're doing because with Braun in the pokey, there's no bear shifter running to your rescue."

"Please," Xandie scoffed. "I'm the hero of my own story." She started down the stairs toward the stage, Lila following.

"Famous last words."

"I'm ignoring you. *La. La. La.*" Xandie stretched when she reached the bottom of the stairs.

"Are you sure you should wear Selena's bracelet? The last two people who had it died, and the other has disappeared."

"Emily ran off, not disappeared, and at least if it's on my wrist, I have it close when the killer takes the bait."

"I'm more worried about the killer taking you out."

"If I were you two girls, I'd be more concerned about what your grandmother's doing working the stage." Amelia, Lila's mother and Xandie's aunt, stood next to the stage and pointed to the spotlight.

Elspeth stood next to Winifred, glaring at her daughter, her hands hidden behind her back. "The director robbed me. I've a perfect singing voice."

Winifred opened her eyes wide and took half a step back. "You do. You definitely do. Much, much better than mine. I don't know what the director was thinking when he hired me." Winifred happily threw Jules under the bus.

Ignoring her daughter, Elspeth opened her arms wide and stepped into the spotlight. "Let Point Muse discover my talent." With a cackle, she winked at Xandie and threw a small water balloon back over her head. It exploded in a plume of purple smoke over Winifred and Cornelius' heads.

"Well, there goes Harrow social life. No one will have us around for fear of hexing," Amelia sniped. "Wait until Miranda hears about Elspeth's antics."

Xandie's mom, Miranda, was the eldest of Elspeth's daughters, with Amelia the middle daughter and Winifred the youngest. Lila's mother was an animal Empath and Vet for the town and the most no-nonsense of all the Harrows. Especially when Elspeth was up to her chaotic, mayhem-loving antics.

"Speaking of Mom, any idea when she and Buchanan will be back from their fact-finding mission?" Buchanan, Elspeth's Paladin Knight boyfriend, and Xandie's mother were the most action-minded of the Harrow clan. No doubt their combined military training would come in handy when taking down the killer.

"Some time tomorrow, before the big MMU rally. That's all I know." Amelia winced as Elspeth trilled a series of discordant notes. "I should've chained her to the bed."

Lila shuddered as Cornelius leapt forward and croaked like a frog. "Best just to let her have her way for a while, rather than wait for the wicked witch to plan her revenge."

Percy's story would go out in a few hours. Tonight, Selena and Polly's politician killer would hopefully read their news story bait. But for now, Xandie needed to spike the gossips' interest. She wanted everyone talking about the murder and the evidence she'd found. Xandie nudged Lila. "Your mother's riding herd on Elspeth and Winifred, and Holly's working at the funeral home. Why don't we go get a pizza at the Santos Brothers' Pizzeria while we wait for the killer to take the bait?"

"Good idea. Operation sneak out it is." Lila backed away slowly from her mother, dragging Xandie with her. Picking up pace, the cousins burst out of the Playhouse into an early Point Muse evening.

Xandie took a deep breath and centered her nerves. A shiver ran through her body. The day had turned crisp and chilly. She breathed in again, enjoying the momentary peace before the storm descended.

"I flat out refuse to have chocolate on our pizza. You hear me, Meyers?"

"Sugar police." Xandie strolled down the pavement with Lila by her side. Pizza would hit the spot, and the heavy dough might even help her sleep instead of worrying about trapping the killer tomorrow. A tall shadow detached itself from a clump of trees on the side of the road. Xandie gripped Lila's arm as the shadow formed into Emma

Matthews. The women sagged in relief. "Emma, you scared us."

The dryad stared vacantly at Xandie for a moment before awareness seeped in. "Librarian. I've been looking for you. The trees told me you'd be here."

Okay, that wasn't the tiniest bit creepy at all. But then, what did she know about dryads? "What can I help you with?"

"You and the Library helped me with my research. I'm going home soon, and I wanted to thank you."

Xandie raised a hand and scratched the back of her neck as it prickled. Emma's eyes tracked the ring of silver on Xandie's wrist. "Have you seen this bracelet before, Emma?" Xandie brought her arm down, and the dryad tracked the movement.

"Yes, my husband bought it for that woman. He's been looking for it."

"I just bet he has," Lila muttered under her breath.

"Will you tell your husband I have it?"

Emma considered Xandie for a moment. "He was angry with Selena and demanded the bracelet back. She laughed at him. He didn't like that because he knew what she was going to do with it. Said he knew her too well. He'd do anything for MMU and the Noe family." Focus faded from her face. "If you want me to, I'll let my husband know you found the bracelet, but you need to be careful. Don't want the Librarian hurt. She might have more books for me." Emma wandered off, muttering to herself.

Xandie strained to hear the words.

"It's the quiet ones you have to watch out for."

"What?"

Lila pointed to Emma. "That's what she said. It's the quiet ones you have to watch out for."

Strange thing to say. Alistair Matthews definitely wasn't quiet. Xandie shucked off her disquiet and put Emma's words down to the tree-obsessed ramblings of a part dryad. She had bigger things to worry about...

Like a chocolate-free pizza and a killer to uncover.

NINETEEN

"If Colin gets any closer to that bonfire, he'll be roasted pug." Xandie winced as Colin pranced forward, taunting a little brownie who brandished a stick at the dog.

"Don't worry about Colin. I give it, *three, two, one...*" Lila pointed at a shrieking Elspeth, who rushed in and snatched up Colin.

"My poor baby. What has that nasty brownie done to you?" Elspeth cooed over her pug and glared at the offending brownie. Sparks reflected around her, and the brownie backed away, hands in the air.

"The wicked witch has still got it." Her grandmother was a hoot. A pain in Xandie's behind, but still a hoot.

"The witch never lost it, considering the number of countries that have banned her from their borders."

Xandie nudged Lila and nodded to the stage where Matthews and his wife were chatting with party members. "The gang's all here."

"Not quite. Good old George, Matthews' shadow, isn't here."

"He'll be lurking somewhere." Xandie peered around

the crowd. Most of Point Muse had turned out for the MMU bonfire rally. Point Muse Springs Resort bordered national forest land. Point Muse sat on a nexus of ley lines and repelled humans. Supernatural creatures loved the remote area. Xandie hugged herself, feeling unsettled. She'd switched Selena's bracelet to her ankle, so it wasn't so prominent, but she still had it on her.

"Nervous? Percy's article went out last night. And Emma hopefully passed on the message to her husband that you had the bracelet. According to Percy, he's never had so many downloads."

Xandie grimaced. "If something's going to happen, it will be at the bonfire. But yeah, I'm nervous. Jasper and his men are wandering around, and every Harrow and their cronies are on alert. I'll be fine. Just nerves."

Lila patted Xandie's back. "It's not just about finding the killer; it's about clearing Braun's name. You're allowed to be titchy."

"Titchy?" Xandie snorted. "Are you borrowing words from Elspeth?"

"Shouldn't we all learn from our elders?" Salvatore Noe bowed to Xandie and Lila. "Glad you could join the rally. It seems like everyone in Point Muse has turned up."

Including Selena's shady, loan-shark brother. "Point Muse residents don't get out much. Any excuse to party."

"MMU will appreciate the support, I'm sure." He smiled charmingly down at Xandie. "How goes the investigation?"

"Bumping along. Hopefully, everything will resolve by the end of the night." Xandie stared challengingly at the Noe family representative. She was positive Matthews was the killer, but Salvatore was a dangerous player.

"I'm sure you're right. Something about fire and mass

gatherings brings out the worst in people." He bowed again and blended back into the crowd.

"That guy gives me the heebie-jeebies." Lila shivered.

"Shake it off. It's almost showtime. You know what to do." Xandie wandered off in the opposite direction as her cousin, weaving through the crowd until she reached the side of the stage.

"I see your grandmother has a hipflask and is dancing around the bonfire."

"At least she isn't naked. It could be far, far worse." Xandie hugged her mother and touched a scrape on the side of Miranda's forehead. "What kind of tussle did you and Buchanan get into?"

Miranda shrugged. "Information gathering can be cutthroat."

"Where's Elspeth's boy toy?"

"Making sure his girlfriend doesn't shed her clothing. He's worried about burns on wrinkled skin."

"I'd be worried about everyone else. Did you find out any information?"

Miranda wrapped an arm around her daughter and lowered her voice so no one would overhear them. "We spoke to one of Buchanan's contacts. The Noe family have no outstanding debts linked to Matthews."

"We found paperwork showing a debt of five hundred grand."

"That's interesting, since they swear the only debt they had on file was from when he was young, and that's already paid in full."

"Why have paperwork for a debt that doesn't exist?"

"Another interesting little tidbit is that Salvatore Noe disappeared from the family compound a few weeks ago. They have no clue where he is or what he's doing. They think he's gone rogue. But they did admit they may have a family asset in play in Point Muse."

Xandie tapped her chin. Selena's brother had dropped off the family radar a week before Selena died. Whatever he was doing was unsanctioned by his family. "I think Matthews borrowed money but from Selena's brother. Maybe he's here to get his payment plus interest back, not to mention avenge his sister's killing?"

"He has a somewhat shady past. Spent various hitches in different institutions growing up."

"Good old Sal isn't as charming as he seems."

"Maybe not. Be careful." Miranda gave Xandie a quick squeeze and let her go. "I want to check out the perimeter and liaise with that detective."

Xandie blew her mother a kiss. After so many years of mourning her, it was nice to have the maternal concern back in her life. Her father did what he could, but the strait-laced librarian couldn't provide maternal backup like a mother could.

Matthews took a step closer to the microphone. "Can everyone hear me?"

Xandie winced and stepped farther back into the shadows as the vibrating feedback from the microphone abused her ears.

Matthews raised his hands for quiet. "Friends and family of MMU. We thank you for coming to our last engagement in the welcoming town of Point Muse. Let's hear it for the township."

Scattered applause sounded from around the bonfire.

"Welcoming except for the murders," Xandie muttered to herself as George slid in next to her with two cups in hand.

"Every town has a downside. Would you like a hot

chocolate? I'm not much of a drinker, so I like to hit the hot chocolate and tea stands." He offered Xandie a cup.

Grabbing the drink, Xandie took a sip gratefully. It was a tad chilly tonight, even with the bonfire. The hot chocolate was a bonus. Even if the chocolate wasn't Lila's, it was still tasty. She swirled the liquid around her mouth as a slightly bitter aftertaste hit her tongue. "Thanks, George."

"It isn't as good as your cousin's. But they used real chocolate to make it."

That explained the bitterness. "It's fine. The MMU is getting ready to move to the next town tomorrow?"

George nodded. "Emma's heading home, but we'll visit the next town. We have a few more days before votes are counted for the council position."

Xandie took another swallow and then yawned. Elspeth darted around the edge of the bonfire, Buchanan in tow, as she called out for Colin. "That annoying pug must've done a runner." Xandie yawned again, eyes heavy. Sleuthing took a toll on her sleep patterns.

"Whoa." George gently took Xandie's drink and placed both cups on the

ground. "Maybe you should head home, get some sleep."

She wavered on her feet, fatigue weighing her eyelids down. Her ears echoed with Elspeth's frantic calls for the missing pug. Maybe Xandie should just have a little nap. It couldn't hurt.

"Can I help you to the resort? You can call someone to come get you." George gently supported Xandie's weight and led her away.

"Just a minute or two. That's all I need."

"Kid, anyone tell you your schnozzle has a foghorn setting?"

Colin's gravelly, smoke-a-pack-a-day tones, along with his tuna-scented breath, slapped Xandie awake.

"Tell me you didn't eat tuna tonight?" Xandie tried to sit up, frowning when she couldn't move her arms from behind her back.

"Chickie, how you solve crimes is beyond me." Colin nudged Xandie with a paw. "Look around, kid. Hope you don't get seasick."

Xandie shook the last vestiges of sleep from her system. Colin was right — they were bumping up and down like in a roller coaster. It was dark where they were, but Xandie just made out the shape of the bed they were sitting on. A nasty bump sent her careening into a wall, a wood paneled one. That, combined with the rising tide of nausea, confirmed her suspicions. "We're on a boat."

"Ding, ding, ding. The lady is a winner. The only prize is getting kidnapped." Colin flopped down next to Xandie. "I can understand your nosy carcass getting snatched. But what has my fit and toned doggy body got to do with murder?"

"Did you see who took you?"

"Ah, no." Colin looked shamefaced. "Someone left a bowl of delectable tuna out. I thought I'd just have a nibble and it'd be fine. Next thing, I'm waking up next to your foghorn."

Hot chocolate. *George.* Matthews had outsmarted her and had his aide take her.

"He drugged my hot chocolate. And I fell for it." Xandie mentally slapped the back of her head. Talk about stupid.

"Slaves to our taste buds." Colin wiggled around on the bedding and grimaced. "Hey, do you feel that?"

"I don't feel anything."

"Exactly, toots. We've stopped. Thank goodness, because when you gotta go..." Colin trailed off and wiggled again.

No. He couldn't. He wouldn't. Xandie squeaked and hopped off the bed just as Colin furiously wriggled before sagging in relief.

"*No.*" Xandie head-butted the door a few times, not wanting to open her mouth to yell in case of noxious fumes. Thankfully, someone opened the door. Xandie rushed forward into fresh air, heaves wracking her slim figure.

"I'm afraid I may have misjudged the dosage for the Valerian Sleeping Draught." George lifted Xandie's hair out of the way.

"It's not that. Colin's banned from tuna. It upsets his stomach." Xandie waited for the rollercoaster in her gut to settle.

George peered worriedly at a grinning pug. "Hopefully, he won't suffer any ill effects. I'm an animal lover at heart." George gently lifted Colin up and linked his arm through Xandie's bound ones. "Upsy daisy, you two. We have a transaction to finish. I've a full schedule tomorrow."

Xandie coughed and cleared her throat. "Don't you mean Matthews? Or do you always do his dirty deeds?"

George shook his head. "Matthews is quite a disappointment, but he does have a vision. One that could be beneficial for my family."

Xandie shook the last of the cobwebs from her brain. "What family?"

"Poor dear. Your sleuthing abilities are quite overestimated, aren't they? You didn't find out that the Noe family changed their name when they first came to American shores? Our original name was Persinoe. They shortened it to Noe, but I like Perse." George grinned with a slightly manic twitch of his lips at Xandie.

Realization hit like a ton of bricks. Emma had been right. It really was the quiet ones you had to watch out for.

TWENTY

She was an idiot. "It was never Matthews, was it?"

George trilled a high-pitched laugh. "Well, I suppose you could say he caused it with his little dalliance with my cousin, Selena."

"I don't suppose you'd consider cutting my hands loose? It's not like I can run away." George had brought Xandie and Colin to a deserted rocky island not too far off Xandie's private beach. The one at the base of the Library, where her great-aunt Sera used to take her to play with the merrows. In fact, if she squinted, she could just make out the outline of her little dock. Except swimming at night with a pug and her hands tied didn't impress her with high survival odds, and then there was George. "Why? Why kill Selena and Polly? Are you that attached to Matthews or is it Emma?"

"You think I'm in love with that vacant-minded dryad? Neither of the Matthews are very appealing, but I'm loyal. To my family. Unlike that mouthy trollop," George cursed, spittle flying.

The guy really didn't like his cousin very much. Xandie shifted against the rock that he'd propped her up against.

He might be a killer, but he wasn't very smart. Sharp rocks equal getting out of ropes. "What did Selena do?"

"If she opened her mouth, she lied and blackmailed. A disgrace on the Noe name."

"Isn't that what your family does? Aren't they the mafia of the sirens?"

George roared and shoved his face into Xandie's. "The Noes took me in when my family couldn't raise me. Correction, they didn't want to raise a talentless leech. The Noes didn't care. They could see my usefulness. Unlike that slanderous siren."

Smart of the family. Taking a distant and unwanted relative and brainwashing him to do all their dirty work. Disposable minion. "What was Selena's plan?"

George pulled back, chest heaving as he fought for control. "She took that damn bracelet and recorded their affair, their fights. Even Matthews taking money from Selena's brother. She was going to turn everything over to the ex-boyfriend, that police chief. The family has too much invested in MMU. I couldn't let that happen."

"You killed Selena."

"It wasn't hard to get my hands on a spelled necklace. She honestly thought it was from that bear. I looked for the bracelet afterward, but Selena's dresser found it instead."

"She blackmailed you and Matthews. I saw someone talking to her outside the conference room. I just didn't realize it was *you*." One rope binding Xandie's hands gave way.

"Selena's dresser was so gullible. None of them expected me to hurt them." He shook his head. "I arranged to meet the dresser backstage. I turned up early and rigged that prop to fail. But I still couldn't find that cursed bracelet."

"She'd already given it to Emily, who freaked out and gave it to me." Xandie smirked. Anything to keep George villain-monologuing. Might give her extra time to work out a plan. She glanced around the small rocky island. There was literally nothing here but rocks and a shifty-eyed pug pacing a few meters away. *Shifty-eyed?* Xandie shuffled her focus around the moonlit island. Colin had seen something or someone. But who? Needing to keep George distracted, Xandie kept talking. "When did you realize I had it?"

"I saw you at the bake sale, coming away from the bathroom. I figured you must've searched Matthews' office. Then I read the article by that Point Muse reporter. I knew you had the evidence, the bracelet. And here we are."

A shadow bobbed near the edge of the rocky island, then ducked out of sight with a flip of a colorful tail. Coral, the merrow, was the only mermaid she knew. The girl had helped her mom and had played with a young Xandie. Maybe help was on the way. "Why take Colin then?" The final rope securing her wrists gave way, but she kept her hands behind her back. The element of surprise.

"He's here to secure your compliance. Give me the bracelet and I leave him untouched. Don't and..." George trailed off menacingly.

"There's one thing I don't understand," Xandie said.

George gave a deep sigh. "What is it? Anything to get this over with."

"How did you get the police chief's fingerprints? They were all over everything."

He chuckled, reached into the pocket of his jacket, and pulled out a bundle of letters that he waved around. "I happened to find these. Letters from your bear that he wrote to that siren when he was at the Academy. She kept them all. It was easy to get someone to create a removal hex to lift his fingerprints and then transfer them to whatever I wanted. A wonderful way to point the finger of blame at someone else. Now, enough of that. Give me the bracelet."

"What happens if I do give it to you? You'll leave us stranded out here or kill us?"

Dropping to his knees, George nodded earnestly. "I really don't want to hurt anyone else. You and the dog are perfectly nice. I'll leave you here and I'm sure someone will spot you in the morning. Just give me the bracelet."

Colin joined the verbal fray. "You know what? I kinda don't want to stay here. I miss my Elspeth." The pug lifted his leg and let loose on George.

Screeching, the killer cartwheeled back. His arms flailed as he tried to avoid the putrid dog spray.

Xandie took advantage of his distraction and grabbed a loose rock, ramming it against the side of George's head. She scooped up Colin and bolted to where she'd seen Coral's tail.

George staggered upright, blood streaming from a slice on his forehead. "I would have let you go, but now—"

Xandie cut him off with a snort. "You were never going to let us go. You just admitted to murdering two people."

"You're right. So now I've no choice but to choke the life out of you myself." He stepped forward, hand outstretched

"Duck," someone roared at Xandie and yanked her and Colin to the ground, shoving earmuffs onto both of them.

Salvatore Noe stood singing, his song lilting and ethereal. George ground to a halt and wavered on his feet, an Emma-style blank look upon his face.

Xandie raised a hand to remove the earmuffs.

"Nope." Braun moved her hand away and shifted Xandie closer to his side. "Elspeth spelled the earmuffs. We can still hear, but the call doesn't affect us."

Jasper made sure Colin's earmuffs stayed on. "She's a firecracker, your grandmother."

Sagging against Braun's side, she considered the bear shifter and his ex- nemesis. All three men were attired in tight black wetsuits. "How did you know?"

"Your mom noticed you and Colin missing. Elspeth tracked you to the docks and the missing boat. The merrows had already worked out what was happening and alerted us." Braun tightened his grip on Xandie.

"Miranda had diving gear, and Salvatore turned up and let us know it was George. Elspeth spelled the muffs and the merrow swam us out," Jasper added.

George jerked as Selena's brother hit a high note, then collapsed to his knees, drool running from a slack mouth.

Looking winded, Salvatore joined them. "It is finished. Selena can rest easy."

"I guess you weren't threatening me?"

He grated out a rusty laugh. "More like trying to warn you, but I'm not used to acting like a good guy."

"I'm sorry about your sister."

He nodded sadly. "She was a siren. There's a reason they call us monsters. George may not have had the gift, but mentally, he was one of us. Everything he did was for the family and the family alone. No matter the cost."

"What do we do with him now?" Xandie nodded to the zombie man staring at nothing.

"I broke his mind, unfortunately. I'm hoping you have the bracelet recording to prove his guilt." He arched an eyebrow.

Xandie cackled, imitating Elspeth, and lifted a leg. The bracelet caught the moonlight. "You betcha. I recorded everything."

Salvatore nodded. "Detective Scott and Paladin Inc are

placing me into witness protection, and I'm turning evidence on my family. The Noe family syndicate is going down."

"Trust us. We won't let this happen to anybody else." Braun ran his hands down Xandie's leg. Shivering, not entirely from the cold, she elevated her leg so he could unclasp the bracelet.

He handed it off to Jasper with a wink.

Seems like those two had repaired their bromance. Xandie wrapped an arm around Zach's waist and hugged tight.

"Sorry to interrupt the hugfest, but what's a pug gotta do to get some vittles around here? I'm starving."

Xandie and the others broke into laughter at the pug's plaintive demands.

"There's no call for laughter. My pee saved the day. I'm a hero."

For once, Xandie agreed. Her hero, her four-legged hero, had saved the day...*with bodily fluids*.

How very Point Muse.

TWENTY-ONE

The fire crackled in Harrow House with a cheerful noise. Xandie snuggled up on the lopsided velvet couch, and the warm bear shifter adjusted her against his side. "Who did you have to bribe to get five minutes of peace for us to finish our date?"

Braun chuckled, and the movement of his muscles against Xandie's head made her bob like a dancing parrot. "I appealed to Elspeth's romantic nature. And the likelihood of zero great-grandchildren without special alone time."

Xandie snorted. "Elspeth doesn't have a romantic bone in her body. What did you really offer her?"

"Cold hard cash, enough fresh honey to drown a bear in, and one get-out-of-jail-free card." Braun lifted Xandie onto his lap.

"You were suckered. She probably would've caved just at the cold hard cash."

Braun shrugged. "I still feel I got the good end of the bargain." He winked at Xandie. "Besides, this is officially the first date that we'll finish."

Xandie raised her head and hovered her lips over his. "What are the odds you're wrong?"

Holly burst into Harrow House, blood on her hands and her eyes shining like silver moons. She tilted her head back and shrieked.

Even Harrow House shuddered at the ferocity of the banshee's wails.

Xandie gritted her teeth and slapped a hand over her ears. "I think you should ask for a refund from Elspeth."

The end.

Want More?
You can sign up for my mailing list. It's for new releases and no spam. Be the first to grab specials, new releases, and freebies.

Sign up now

https://www.kellyethan.com/newsletter

LEAVE A REVIEW

Did you like this book?

Please leave a review for it on Amazon!

The Slanderous Siren and the Grievous Gift

ABOUT THE AUTHOR

I want to thank everyone who spent the time to read my
novel.

My world is small town magic, mystery and mayhem, with
plenty of snarky laughs along the way.

With an overactive imagination and a love of all things that
go bump in the night, it was natural to write cozy
paranormal mysteries, but I also love paranormal romance.
No matter the genre, I love sarcastic heroines who like to
save the day and solve the puzzle.

With a busy and chaotic household, writing is my outlet for
madness. I live in Australia and when not writing, I can be
found plotting my next fictional murder or chasing after the
family's ferocious hellhound.

Visit me today at my website or say hello on social media.

Website:
https://www.kellyethan.com

facebook.com/KellyEthanWriter

instagram.com/kellyethanauthor

tiktok.com/@authorkellyethan

COZY PARANORMAL MYSTERY:

Point Muse Cozy Paranormal Mystery Series

The Wicked Witch and the Christmas Chaos
The Wicked Witch and the Stolen Snow Globe
The Conniving Carver and the Jeering Jack-O Lantern
The Wicked Witch and the Ultimate Smackdown
The Wicked Witch and the Abominable Snowman
The Wicked Witch and the Killer Grinch

#0 The Pernicious Pixie and the Choked Word
#1 The Killer Knight and the Murderous Chairleg
#2 The Dastardly Dragon Killer and the Poisoned Breath
#3 The Murderous Monster and the Stony Gaze
#4 The Cursed Crow and the Deadly Hex
#5 The Slanderous Siren and the Grievous Gift
#6 The Vengeful Villain and the Cursed Treasure
#7 The Fiendish Foe and the Deadly Jewels
#8 The Nefarious Nemesis and the Wedding Jinx

Point Muse Cozy Paranormal Mystery Boxed Set: Books 1-3

Point Muse Cozy Paranormal Mystery Boxed Set: Books 4-6

Point Muse Cozy paranormal Mystery Boxed Set: Books 1-8

LILA HARROW: Point Muse Cozy Paranormal Mystery

Cookies, Curses and Christmas Corpses.

#1 Cupcakes, Corpses and Chaos

#2 Pies, Potions and Peril

#3 Sin, Sugar and Shadows

LILA HARROW Point Muse Boxed Set: Books 1-3

HOLLY HARROW: Point Muse Cozy Paranormal Mystery

Banshee, Vikings and Voodoo

#1 Banshee, Death and Disarray

#2 Banshee, Moonshine and Madness

#3 Banshee, Sea Monster and Sabotage

HOLLY HARROW Point Muse Boxed Set: Books 1-3

The Ghost Vein Mine Cozy Paranormal Mysteries

#1 Ghosts and Gold Dust

#2 Curses and Cold Cases

Non Fiction

Heart and Craft.